TOO FAR

Rich Shapero

Outside
Reading

San Mateo, California

Outside Reading
P.O. Box 1565
San Mateo, CA 94401

Library of Congress Cataloging-in-Publication Data is available.

ISBN: 978-0-9718801-4-6

Cover painting by Eugene Von Bruenchenhein, *EVB #191*
(for more information, visit www.vonbruenchenhein.com)
Artwork copyright © 2009 Rich Shapero
Title font and additional graphics: Sky Shapero
Cover design: Adde Russell
Map art: Laurie Lipton www.laurielipton.com
Author photo: Henry Boxer

Printed in the UK by CPI William Clowes Beccles NR34 7TL

15 14 13 12 11   1 2 3 4 5

Also by Rich Shapero

Wild Animus

1

On the outskirts of Fairbanks, down a gravel road, a small house and a family had taken root among the trees. A man and a woman, and a six-year-old boy. They had come from a long distance, impelled by an idea, like seed flock on the wind. In May the northern sky pales early. Dreams trail off, and you wake and dress yourself. Robbie, the boy, managed that himself now.

After they ate breakfast, Dad would leave. Robbie would go outside.

Between the house and the wilds was a bald spot—the Clearing—and there he sat this particular morning, in deep concentration.

Is the stick curious or something to fear?

He was twiddling a dry twig between stones, and down in the pocket a spider was watching.

Does it have a mind of its own? Robbie thought, as the spider might. *Or is someone holding it? Following everything I do.* Like a voice from the heavens, he spoke to the spider. "Grab on—"

Light steps crossed the Clearing. In his circle of sight: one shoe, then two. Socks bright and unmatched—one purple, one blue.

Robbie looked up. A girl, his own age.

"Is someone down there?" she asked.

Her eyes seemed enormous. But it wasn't their size. Fervent thoughts, and wild ones, were churning inside. She had a brown pony tail spouting over one ear. Over the other, locks were twisted oddly, ribboned and knotted with rubber bands.

"Yep," Robbie answered. "I'm his friend."

She bent over and saw the spider. Her head tilted, as if considering how to introduce herself. Then she began to hum. A lilting melody—something you might please yourself with when no one else was around. Robbie listened as he peered between the stones. The song seemed to speak to him as well. There was a call to freedom in it, a confidence that banished care.

"Hey," Robbie said. "He's climbing out."

The girl smiled, spread her arms with a theatrical flourish and rose. Then, without a word, she began to turn. Her hands trailed, as if letting go of something. There was a magenta scarf around her shoulders and a scarlet one at her waist, and they flared as she whirled, faster and faster. She closed her

2

eyes and her attention drew into a private quarter. Robbie was mesmerized.

The girl stopped and plunked down beside him.

Robbie felt their knees touch.

"Everything's loose," she laughed, making a dizzy face.

Her breath quivered between her lips. A ringlet bounced beside her temple. She was closing her eyes again. Beneath her dark brows, the lids twitched like wings.

"I'm entering the special place," she said.

Robbie heard an invitation.

"Are *you*?"

"Sure," he answered, shutting his eyes.

"The wind sings my songs," the girl said. "So do the leaves. I show them how."

Robbie tried to imagine how you could do that.

"Your turn," she said.

"Okay . . ." Robbie tried to think. "I can write my name backwards." He frowned. *What's so special about that?* He cracked his lids.

She was still immersed. "When I smile, the whole world feels warm," she said.

That's something, Robbie thought, closing his eyes again. "I fly in my dreams."

"I can be as invisible as air," the girl said. "In real life."

"When my friends are in danger, I rescue them."

She giggled. "No one remembers what I remember."

"I go anywhere in the forest," Robbie said. "And I never get lost."

3

He felt a bump. She was shaking him. When he opened his eyes, her face was inches away.

"Really?"

He just stared back.

She turned to the slope behind them. It rose steeply, thronged with aspens and red currant. Buds were starting to burst and the branches were sparked with green. "Have you been up there?"

"Sure." Robbie shrugged, his power leaking away. The Hill was no man's land, as distant and unreachable as the sky above it. He could hear Mom at the back of his mind. *Lying again.*

"I want to see." The girl's eyes flashed.

Robbie nodded.

"Let's go," she said.

Robbie peered back between the stones.

"*Now.*" She stood. "What's your name?"

"Robbie." He rose uncertainly, glancing at his home. It was double trouble. The Hill was forbidden, and the girl would quickly realize that it was a mystery to him.

Her eyes wandered up the slope. "I bet no one has ever been."

Robbie laughed. She was starting through the scrub. Without thinking, he hurried after her. "What's yours?"

She grasped his hand. "Fristeen." Her lips touched his ear.

They reached the first tall tree. Robbie stopped and turned half-around. They both looked at his house.

"Is that where you live?"

4

He nodded. How many hours had he stood by the window wondering what the great story of the forest was about? He gazed up the slope. This was the doorway he couldn't think beyond.

Fristeen's eyes were like the jets on a stovetop, and when she faced him it was like someone had turned the knob all the way. She knew it was forbidden, but she didn't care. And suddenly he didn't either. It was time.

"Don't tell," he said, squeezing her hand.

She promised with a squint. "I love secrets."

They entered the thick shrubs. The twigs had dark skin and brown fingers with bumps at the ends that clawed and caught at them as they passed. The leaf litter hissed and slid beneath them. It was a strange new world for Robbie, and there was another strange world clasping his hand. It was warm and alive, and not the least bit hesitant or ill-at-ease. There was a rhythm in Fristeen's breath, in her step, and inside her. And when her fingers wriggled, it was as if she spoke. "Look at this, look at that." Tips of life peering up at them, lime and maroon. Flowers venturing up from the matted litter, some quailing, some headstrong. A wasps' nest, glaring through the branches like an ashen face.

"Feel," Fristeen said as they neared a big tree. She reached out, and he did the same. Its skin was gray, cool and smooth.

"Listen." Robbie closed his eyes.

"Do you hear something?" she wondered.

"His thoughts," Robbie whispered. "He has a secret in his fingers. Look, up there." He pointed.

From a branch, twigs spoked like an unclenched fist, and leaves were trembling at the end of each.

"They're thinking—all of them. See?" Robbie swept the slope. "Thinking about leaves!"

Fristeen yelped and broke into a run.

She reached a bush. Robbie was right behind her. She grabbed its fingers and pinched its buds, and its leaves jumped out. "Look." Robbie spun around to another. "Shiny." Then on to another and up the slope, running back and forth from bough to bole. Some buds were sharp, some were still hard. But most were excited, swollen and ready, and when your fingers squeezed, they burst for joy. Green ones, gray ones, some pink like flesh. Some fuzzy, some silky, some big and sticky with a minty smell.

The trees upslope were clamoring. So they raced to the next, Fristeen crying, "You can't stop between." Some leaves bristled, some fanned, some you had to unroll. Look—red. No, silly, it's your fingers showing through. And then they were guessing before they popped the buds. Furry— Prickly! Purple, I bet.

All of a sudden, there wasn't any more Hill. They whirled and hooted and jumped up and down. Robbie ran to the tallest aspen, threw his arms around it and looked straight up. The gray branches reached—nothing between them and the sky. The tree was urging him to climb.

Fristeen was beside him, red-faced, breathless.

"I could," Robbie gasped. "I think I could."

"I know you could. Look," she pointed down the slope.

6

It was an amazing sight. Robbie's house was so small you could pick it up with your fingers.

He struggled with a new perspective. "I was there all the time." He glanced at Fristeen. "I never left."

"When I was a baby, I was in prison—a wooden jail. That's what Grace says."

"Grace?"

"Come on." Fristeen turned from the slope, faced the forest beyond and started forward.

Robbie didn't follow.

She looked back. "It's okay."

"Yeah, but—"

"What?"

He heard the disappointment in her voice. "I've been that way before," he said.

"You have?"

Robbie swallowed. The breezes had vanished and the woodland was silent, awaiting his response. "I don't want to lie to you," he said.

She gave him a fond look.

"Let's go back," he said.

She shook her head.

"You'll be scared."

"Oh, I know," Fristeen said with relish.

That stopped him. Was it a bluff? No, he could see the truth in her smile: she exulted in things that frightened her. A stray breeze sent a chill up Robbie's back. He shivered, feeling himself in the presence of something new and strange.

Across the space that separated them, her gaze met his darkly, boldly.

"Fristeen," he murmured. Was he reasoning with her or pleading? As long as he could remember, his head had been full of fantasies. Lies, Mom called them. For all his rich imagination, he lacked the daring to make anything of them. The answer was staring him in the face.

"I might need someone to rescue me," she said.

Retreat seemed suddenly unworthy. This was the Hill, the great unknown. And here he was on top of it, feeling its freedom along with its fear. Fristeen made him think he could be master of both.

"You might," Robbie nodded, stepping toward her.

The earth dipped and turned lumpy. They headed into a patch of thin trees that were all bent over. When Robbie glanced at Fristeen, she was too.

"Follow the Bendies," she said with a secret look.

Robbie laughed and hunched.

They reached a place where the trees had snapped and lay piled on top of each other. There was an open space beneath, and they got down on their hands and knees and crawled through.

"Wait," Robbie said as they rose. He lifted his hand and pulled at one of her ribbons. The braid untwisted, covering her eye. When he brushed the hair aside, his fingertips skimmed her brow.

"What are you doing?" she asked softly.

He turned and tied the ribbon to an overhanging branch. "Marking the way."

Fristeen's eyes grew wide. "So you don't get lost." Kids did that in fairytales.

Robbie nodded. Would it work? They'd find out on the way back.

The spell of fairytale was, in fact, stealing over them both. You're listening, and it all seems so unlikely—full of peculiar places and things that could never happen. And then all at once, you're in the middle of it, burning to know what will come next and believing every bit of it.

They crossed a bed of dead leaves and whisked through parched grass. Strange signs appeared, half-buried in the soil. A shovel head. A section of pipe. A rusty can. Relics of some ancient people. Then the earth ended abruptly. At the verge, a large rusted barrel lay on its side with its open end toward them, and beyond that, a stream wandered between steep walls. On the opposite bank, a dark visage loomed.

Where a large willow had bent, you could see the vault of a brow and a face netted with dead branches. Shocks of hair rayed to either side. A nexus of twigs formed a piercing eye. The other was narrowed, as if considering. Beneath the collapsed willow, where the bank had been hollowed, a wetness glossed giant lips, and roots emerged around it.

"His beard," Robbie said, pointing.

"Hear, hear, hear . . ." A voice echoed from the rusty drum.

"And ears," Fristeen said.

"And a nose."

"He Knows," the face said. "He Knows, He Knows . . ."

The mass of dark branches squinted and stared.

"He Knows," Robbie whispered. "That's his name."

They traded glances. If He Knows really knew—

Robbie peered over the edge. "Where does it go?" he asked.

"The stream," Fristeen added.

"Dream," He Knows replied, "dream, dream, dream . . ."

"I'm in the mood," she said.

"Too, too, too . . ."

"Would we get back," Robbie asked, "before dark?"

"Far, far, far, far . . ."

Robbie searched the rim. To the left, where the banks pinched together, a fallen aspen bridged the stream. On the far side, the way rose through the brush.

Fristeen started along the rim.

"Okay." Robbie followed.

"Wait, wait, wait . . ."

They looked at each other. Fristeen grabbed Robbie's hand.

"You're an old troll," she cried.

"Cold, cold, cold . . ."

"No, it's not," Robbie shouted.

"Fog, fog, fog . . ."

They headed toward the fallen aspen, kicking up litter, shoes sucking in mud as the gurgle of the flow rose in their

ears. The log's gray skin was patterned with moss. They straddled it and scooted across. On the far side, they started up a
long slope. They were both breathing hard when they reached
the top. A ridge rose on the right, dipped and then lifted still
higher. Everything seemed to slope down from that crest. It
made you dizzy, just looking at it.

"Do you think we should?"

Robbie saw the foreboding in Fristeen's eyes. His dread
surfaced, along with the memory of her bravado at the top of
the Hill. It was crazy—the impulse to hurl yourself at something you feared. "Dare you," he said, and he started up.

"No!" Fristeen hurried forward with shrieks and cries,
jubilant.

The dry growth had been flattened by wind or snow. At
the dip were twin stumps that you stepped between. Then the
pitch grew steeper. They held hands, huffing as they climbed.
What had happened here? The slopes on either side were naked. Was it safe to look down? Not yet, not yet. Then you did,
and what you saw were the tops of trees, all thin and bony
with dead leaves beneath—a speckled brown sky with tiny
green stars.

It was exciting, but frightening. You put your face into the
wind and you didn't talk. It was that kind of place. The forest
around you expanded with every step.

So many, Robbie thought. Uncountable. Below and beyond, far into the distance— It was all one big tangle of trunks
and arms. Vast, endless. Maybe this was why grownups said
scary things about the deep woods, and got nervous when you

asked. It was something they preferred not to think about. How could you be anything but lost in a world like this?

"Robbie?"

He glanced over his shoulder.

"If we fell off—"

"You can't," he said. He stopped. "Stay where you are."

He took a few more steps. Then he closed his eyes and let his knees buckle. He landed on his rear in the soil. When he looked back she was laughing. Then she hopped forward and sat down beside him.

It wasn't the highest point on the ridge, but it was a privileged place. They scanned the valleys, and for what seemed a long time, silence prevailed. Finally Fristeen spoke.

"When Dada plays his guitar, I don't talk. Just like this."

A breeze passed between them.

"Mine's going to be a doctor," Robbie said.

"He wants to help people."

"Not that kind. Do you know what you're going to be?"

Fristeen smiled to herself. "I'm going to be the sun."

Her cheek brushed his. He could smell her hair. It was sweet and smoky, honey melting in tea with a fire going.

"What about you?"

Robbie shook his head. "I'll figure it out in first grade." He shivered. The air seemed suddenly colder.

"You're going to school?"

"When summer's over. Aren't you?" Something shifted at the corner of Robbie's eye. White scarves were rising out of the ravines just below.

"If I want to spell something, Grace shows me how."

The scarves were connecting into misty chains, climbing with such speed that it was easy to imagine they had some purpose.

"We better go back," he said.

Fristeen saw the alarm in his eyes.

In front of them and behind, giant white fingers crept over the ridge.

As they stood, a huge snarl of mist rose with them, sending tendrils out, circling their bodies like icy rope. They shivered through them, waving their arms to clear a view of the crestline and hurrying down. As quickly as they moved, the vapors followed. Others appeared, swimming from either side, anticipating their flight. Would they make it down the ridge before— No, coiling vapors were drifting together below, meeting and joining to seal the way.

Robbie stumbled. He rolled over and stopped abruptly as his knees struck something woody. Fristeen cried out, grabbing his shoulder, trying to keep him from the invisible depths below. Robbie drew his feet beneath him, then saw the problem: one of his shoes was unlaced. A sharp wind cut through them, and then it was twisting and twisting. He shuddered as he fumbled and his shoe came off. He watched it whirl away into the bottomless fog, hearing He Knows' warning, "Cold, cold, cold."

Chill vapors circled as they stood, and the ridgeline disappeared. Robbie shivered and hobbled forward, feeling his way. The wind tugged the mist tightly around them.

"To the left," a wheezy voice said.

Robbie stopped, glancing back at Fristeen. Her eyes were wide.

He edged to the left, squinting through the blasts. They were descending, leaving the crest, heading straight into a white morass.

"Put your best foot forward," the invisible voice said.

Robbie recoiled and began side-stepping up the incline. As they regained the crest, the voice came again.

"Almost, almost—" A crazy titter ricocheted around them.

"Who are you?" Fristeen demanded.

"The future," came the answer from deep in the fog. The blast beat at them, shaking their parts. "Shivers, for now."

Robbie peered at the whorls, then gripped Fristeen. There were sockets for eyes and soggy cheeks below. A sagging nose. A scud curdled like a rumpled brow.

"Whatever brings you here?"

"We're exploring," Fristeen said.

"Without coats?" An O opened between Shivers' cheeks, and through it a freezing wind blasted.

Robbie flung his arm around Fristeen, fearful they would be swept from the ridge.

The cloudy presence stood between them and safety. Was that a high collar? No, a chin impossibly long, wound around his neck.

"What do you want?" Robbie shouted.

"Want?" Shivers blustered. He began to quake. The turmoil mounted in his throat, as if he was choking, then his

14

lips sputtered, "Food!" and the blast was driven with a terrible hacking. "I'm famished." The cloudy jaws chewed. "Children are best."

An eddy reached out, gripping Fristeen like a quivering claw. She screamed. Robbie kept hold of her, shouldering into the maw of the horrid face.

"Doubts, my boy?" Shivers mouthed him. "It's doubt I taste."

Shudders raked their bodies, gums soft and slick wetting them through and spewing them out, delivering them to a frenzy of icy gusts that crossed the ridge like giant razors. Robbie stumbled forward, dragging Fristeen along, a putrid smell clinging to them, trailing back into the guts of the fog.

"Doubt and despair, and the sweet nibble of decay."

Robbie waved his arms to loosen the mist. "The stumps—" He gestured toward the gate where the ridge dipped. They struggled through the flurries while Shivers whispered in their ears.

"Can you see? A feast. In your honor it's laid. At the head of the table, that's me. I chew, I digest, I belch, I void. Romance you seek, and romance you'll find. Hear? Do you hear? All those voices lifted together— Whistling caeca. Buzzing livers. Lungs blown with mold. Glorious—and *you're there.* I hear you both in the swelling choir. Your tiny pipes join mankind's longed-for esperanto. Hyphae ending! Mulch to all! Shivers' peace worldwide."

A break in the fog—the twin stumps stood clear. They raced toward them, but as they approached a shred of mist appeared, hanging between, sagging and furred. One leg was crookt, one arm was raised. And a smudge like a head lifted to face them.

"Get out of our way," Robbie cried. Fristeen was shivering behind him, clutching his waist.

"I'm a patient sort," Shivers' voice creaked with age. "But not for such as you." A tendril lifted like a finger and quivered threateningly at Fristeen.

Robbie looked up and his heart rose in his chest. A lake of fog was suspended directly above them. "Take me, not her." And he hurled Fristeen through the gate.

The hanging figure dissolved as the dam broke, and the freezing white lake came pouring down. And with it, the voice, husky with omen and creaking with scorn.

"Both, and soon. You hear? Both, and soon! It's the short way to Shivers if the heart is your guide."

Robbie dove through the gate. He collided with Fristeen and they crumpled and rolled. Then they were up together, racing down the long slope. Robbie skipped and squawked, sharp things poking through the mulch at his shoeless foot.

They reached the stream, crossed the log bridge and followed the bank. Was Shivers right behind? There—Fristeen's ribbon. They scrambled beneath the Fallen Down Trees, and when they rose, the Bendies were just as they had left them.

At the top of the Hill, the fierce wind vanished abruptly, replaced by a gentle breeze. The spell seemed to dissolve, and their panic subsided.

Far below, Robbie saw his home. The sky hadn't yet dimmed, but the windows were lit. Down they ran, Fristeen headlong, Robbie hobbling. About halfway, she shouted, "Tree to tree." So they zigged and zagged, wheeling and slapping the cool gray trunks. Then the Clearing was before them and they stumbled onto the flat, laughing and hugging and gazing back up the slope.

"We did it," Robbie said. His voice was tremulous. Fristeen's hands were still shaking. Their eyes met, sharing their relief and the narrow escape.

How much had they imagined? Robbie pictured himself recounting the adventure to Mom and Dad. Were they just lies—more elaborate ones? No. What had happened was real. He'd pierced the forbidden without help or permission. Fear had lost its tyranny over him. Fristeen was beside him now, putting her hand in his, grateful and adoring.

"He Knows was right," Robbie said, mastering his pride.

Fristeen agreed.

Robbie faced his home and sniffed. "Hungry?" He could usually tell what was for dinner, but the air was odorless.

"Starving," Fristeen said.

He wasn't. He felt full, not just in his stomach, but in his chest and his head, and his arms and legs, too. It was her, Robbie realized. He was full of Fristeen.

"Want to know something?" He took a breath.

Fristeen saw the look in his eyes.

Robbie struggled for words. "I've got a secret."

She danced in front of him, circled him with her arms and put her lips to his cheek. "No you don't."

Robbie stood speechless, watching as she stepped away from the Clearing and started through the shrubs. Just before she vanished, she turned half around.

"I live right over there," she called back to him, pointing.

2

Robbie saw a shadow in the window. Then the back door burst open and Mom came flying out. Her coat was on, and she had her keys in her hand. She crossed the deck and swept him up, hugging him tightly.

"Mom," he murmured. Her chest was heaving against his, and Robbie could feel the dampness on her cheeks. He drew her plushy scent in and a sigh escaped him. The only true fearlessness was here, in Mom's arms. Robbie was suddenly aware of the tension inside him. He was ticking like a wind-up toy. "Dad?"

His father stepped beside them.

"What are you doing home?"

"Your mom called." Dad put his arm around him.

Robbie grinned and reached out, full of his achievement. "Guess what—"

Mom lost her balance and was forced to let go.

Robbie slid to the deck. "Dad—"

"Where were you?" Mom shrieked. She fell to her knees, eyes wild, grabbing his shoulders and shaking him. Suddenly her face buckled, the accumulated worry overcame her and she was convulsed with sobs. "Where?" she shrieked again.

Robbie tried to find his voice. He could see Mom's lips trembling. "In the Clearing."

"That's a lie," she said.

"And up the Hill." Robbie met her glare.

"You disappeared," Trudy said. The day sitter stepped forward, allying with Mom.

Robbie wrinkled his nose at her.

Mom didn't notice. She'd turned her wrath on Trudy. "I'm ready to fire you."

Trudy bowed her head.

"Are you alright?" Mom asked. "Your shirt's torn. Where *exactly* did you go?"

Robbie saw Dad watching him. There was a hint of sympathy in Dad's eyes. But why was the corner of his mouth lifting? Dad nodded to him, acknowledging his predicament, then he turned and headed back to the house.

At the sound of his footsteps, Mom stiffened. "That's it, Robbie."

He could hear the dejection mixed with her fury.

"You're not leaving the house," Mom said. "Your outside time is over."

Robbie wrenched free. "I don't care," he said. Then he turned like Dad had and strode across the deck.

Dad was on the sofa, thumbing a notebook, his daypack beside him.

"Dad— I climbed the Hill."

"Congratulations." Dad put the notebook down, glancing at the back door. When Robbie reached his knee, Dad roughed his hair and kissed his temple.

"Guess what I saw."

Dad's dark eyes glinted, entering for a moment the spirit of the adventure. "What?"

"There's a stream with a voice, and a place where—"

"You've lost a shoe," Dad laughed.

Robbie looked down. The sight of his muddy sock made him giggle. "Do you have to go back?"

"I think I'm done for the day." Dad eyed the back door again.

"It was scary. This mist came and—"

"Robbie—"

The doorknob was turning.

"Why did you leave the Clearing?" Dad asked.

Mom entered with a much-chastened Trudy.

"I decided to."

"You know the rules," Dad said.

"I was exploring."

Mom leveled her gaze at him. "You *don't* go into the forest alone."

"I *wasn't*—"

Mom's eyes narrowed. "Who were you with?"

"No one."

Dad moved his daypack and Mom sat beside him.

"You broke the rules," Dad said. "What should we do?"

"Nothing," Robbie said. "The rules are stupid."

Mom bristled, but before she could speak, Dad lifted his hand to calm her.

"Robbie—" Dad laughed, leaning forward.

Robbie saw the dark eyes regarding him. What was Dad thinking? Sometimes you could tell—his thoughts were right there in front of you. But sometimes it was the other way. His thoughts were distant and his expression gave no clue. Dad's hair was black, and when stubble shadowed his face, it was that much harder.

"You promised," Dad said.

"I was a little boy then. I'm six now." Robbie smiled. "It's okay."

"We'll decide that," Mom said.

"Well—" Dad sighed.

Robbie could see shadows shifting at the back of Dad's mind.

"Maybe it *is* okay," Dad said softly.

Mom turned scarlet.

Robbie beamed.

Dad took a breath. "Felicia—"

Mom rose, shook her head, and stepped into the kitchen.

For a moment, Dad was lost in thought. Robbie remained silent. The only sound was Mom, cursing and banging pans.

Finally, Dad spoke. "You have to say you're sorry. That's how this works."

Robbie nodded.

"You're the most important thing in the world to her."

Again Robbie nodded.

"Go wash up. I'll come and get you," Dad told him.

They crossed the living room together. Dad motioned to Trudy. She had gathered her things and was waiting by the front door. "Don't worry," he said as Robbie started down the hall. "We'll figure it out. Everything will be fine."

From his room, Robbie heard only the swells of emotion. He couldn't make out what they were saying. They were mad at each other, of course. That didn't bother him. He found a pair of shoes and socks, shut himself in the bathroom and switched on the fan.

First he peed. Then he climbed up, put his muddy foot in the sink and turned on the tap. The cold water made him shudder, and the terrible face swam before him.

Doubts, my boy? Shivers sneered.

Robbie shook his head to banish the phantom. *My boy, my boy*— Shivers, or the thought of him, had followed him home.

"I'm not your boy," Robbie muttered, scrubbing his foot.

He turned off the water, climbed back down and put the fresh footwear on. Then he stood and regarded himself in the mirror.

It was the same face he'd looked at that morning. More serious, maybe. Freedom had done that. His life seemed so much larger now. He combed his hair. It was dark brown, like Fristeen's. His eyes were blue—not a luminous sky blue, like hers. Grayish blue. When would he see her again? There were freckles on his cheeks and his ears stuck out, but there was nothing to be done about that. Maybe tomorrow. The first of his baby teeth had wiggled free the week before. He smiled at the mirror and pushed his tongue into the hole. Then he put his finger on his cheek where Fristeen had kissed it.

They're done now, Robbie thought.

But when he left the bathroom, they were still arguing. So he snuck out of his room and crept along the hall.

Mom was saying something about a moose.

"How many times have we been over this?" Dad said.

"You trust his judgment?"

"He knows what to do," Dad said. "They don't stalk kids."

"Or a bear—"

"The chance of that—" Dad began.

"What if he gets lost?" Mom's voice rose. "What if he falls? What if he breaks his leg—"

"Felicia—"

Robbie pictured the disbelief on Dad's face.

"Stan's boy is six," Dad said, "and he's free as a bird. You ought to get to know Jenny—"

"Once was enough."

"Stan said she enjoyed the morning you spent—"

"Greasing her well pump?" Mom said. "Next time we'll shovel out her privy."

Silence.

"There are a lot of boys Robbie's age," Dad said, "wandering these forests. That's what this is all about."

"For you, not for Robbie."

"He has to take some risks," Dad said.

"Please—don't tell me about Illinois."

"He's got a mind of his own." Dad laughed and repeated in a squeaky voice, "'I was *exploring.*'"

Robbie heard the admiration in Dad's voice.

"I'm glad he isn't content to twiddle around in the Clearing." Dad's scorn filled their small home.

More silence.

"You're turning him against me, Jack."

Mom was faltering.

"The look on his face—" Mom cut herself off.

She was getting sad.

"It's my fault," Mom said. "This never would have happened if I'd been here."

Dad said nothing.

"I'm gone all the time," Mom said.

"Three days a week?"

"It's too much."

"That's insane," Dad said.

Silence again.

"Oh, Jack—"

Robbie could barely hear her now.

"He's changed," Mom said.

"He's your son."

"With work— And school in September—"

Robbie turned and headed back to his room.

"I'm losing him," Mom said.

⟡

When dinner was ready, Dad came to get him.

"Say you're sorry. Remember."

But Robbie did better than that. He circled the table and pulled out Mom's chair for her. It made them both laugh.

"I'm sorry." And he meant it. He loved Mom.

The food wasn't special, but he ate everything on his plate. Afterward, they would talk and agree to change the rules, and there wouldn't be any more arguing.

They cleared the dishes and sat back down. Nothing remained on the table except the two waxen cylinders, white and unlit.

"We set the boundary at the Clearing," Mom said, "when you were five. You're older now. You have better judgment. You can climb the Hill—you've proven that. So we're changing the rules." She glanced at Dad. "You can go to the top of the Hill."

"But—"

Dad's expression warned him.

Robbie shook his head. The new rule didn't make any sense. "There's a place higher up—Where You Can See—"

"If you think the limits should be changed," Dad said, "we'll talk about it. Give it a little time. Alright?" He winked.

"Alright."

"You got Trudy in trouble today," Dad said.

"I know."

"And Mom was really upset. They just want to know where you are."

Robbie nodded.

"The top of the Hill. No farther," Mom said. "I should be able to see you from the deck."

"We won't."

The words slipped out before Robbie could stop them.

"We?" Mom prickled with fresh alarm.

"Me and—" Robbie shrugged and grabbed his milk. "Any friends of mine."

"You were with someone."

Robbie took a swallow. "Yep." He set his glass down.

His indomitable air had its effect. Mom's jaw dropped. Dad tried to straighten his laugh with his hand.

"Well, who was it?" Mom asked.

"Fristeen," Robbie said, pointing through the window. "She lives over there."

Mom's head bowed. "What next?"

Robbie waited for her to continue, but she just sat there. Dad leaned back from the table with a blank look on his face. *What's happening?* Robbie wondered. Dad's attention shifted. He reached for the mail and began to thumb through it.

"She's—" Robbie searched for a word. "Amazing."

"That's beside the point," Mom sighed.

"It had to happen," Dad said under his breath.

"What do you mean? What's wrong?"

"I want you to stay away from her," Mom said.

"But—"

"No 'buts.'"

"You don't under—"

"We've lived next door to them for two years, Robbie. There's a reason I haven't taken you over to play."

"You don't understand—"

"*No,*" Mom said. "You have other friends."

"Fristeen isn't just a—"

"*No,*" Mom repeated sternly.

"I'm going to marry her," Robbie exclaimed.

Mom was dumbstruck.

Dad looked from the mail to Mom. "Did we get an invitation?"

The humor pierced her bewilderment. She made a dazed face and rolled her eyes. "Until then," Mom laughed, "you're not to play with her. Are we clear?"

"But—"

"Are we clear?"

Dad nodded. "Mom's right," he said.

⌒〜

When it was bedtime, Dad came in to read him a story. Robbie was sitting with his back against the pillow and his legs beneath the sheets, sulking.

"What's wrong?" Dad said.

"You know."

Dad's hands shot out. Robbie crowded his arms together, but Dad's fingers found the gaps, playing his ribs like a toy piano.

Robbie howled and writhed till he cried.

When they had both calmed down, Dad pulled a book from the shelf.

"Right here, Doc," Robbie patted the bed.

Dad laughed and sat beside him. "It'll be awhile."

Robbie closed one eye, as if taking aim, pointing his finger in his father's face. "Your brain is a forest."

"And the nerves are trees," Dad sang out.

"When the branches touch—" Robbie brought his forefingers together.

"Snaps jump between the leaves!"

They squinted at each other, and then Dad opened the book.

Robbie put his hand over the title page. "I want to go to the lab."

"Sure."

"And look through the microscope."

"At . . . anything in particular?"

Robbie looked at the wall opposite. A large poster hung there, showing a brain in cross-section. It was ringed with examples of branching nerves. The riddle of the mind—that was an interest he and Dad shared.

"Thoughts travel around inside nerves," Robbie said. "I've seen nerves in the lab. I want to see thoughts."

Dad frowned.

"It's not that simple," Robbie guessed.

Dad shook his head. "Nerves and chemicals are physical mechanisms. They produce thoughts. But we can't see them."

"When you're older, you decide what thoughts you're going to have." Robbie regarded him. "Don't you?"

"What do you mean?"

"Mine just fly out of nowhere. Because I'm six. Right?"

"You'll have more control over them when you're older. But thoughts are that way. They come and go without permission. They can surprise you. Shock you. Overpower you. The way they take control of the mind is a great mystery." He paused. "Is this about the Hill?"

Robbie peered into Dad's eyes. He didn't have to say anything. Dad's eyes were razor sharp, and in their depths the darkness was irising open.

"Thought takes us to our limits," Dad said softly. "The highest mountains, the deepest oceans— And beyond, into the cosmos. To distant galaxies and boundless space. Thought seeks the unknown."

"Exploring," Robbie said.

"Yep." Dad put his arm around Robbie and held him close.

"Mom doesn't understand."

Dad didn't reply. He gazed at the open book for what seemed a long time. Sometimes a thought takes hold of you and won't let go.

"She does understand," Dad said finally. "You don't re-member what it was like in California— And before you were born—" He stopped cold.

"What?"

Dad shook the thought off. "The moose that killed that boy in Nenana— That scared her. It scared me, too."

"He was feeding it peanut butter sandwiches."

Dad eyed Robbie sadly. "Mom would do anything for you. We're lucky to have her. Don't make things harder for her."

"Just tell me why."

"Why what?"

"Why she doesn't like Fristeen."

"Let's not get into that."

"Has she ever met her?"

"Probably not."

"What about you?"

Dad shook his head. "I bet she's a firecracker."

Robbie laughed, and a little star burst to life between Dad's mind and his.

"Now listen—" Dad turned serious. "The rules may be nonsense. But you better use your head. Even great explorers make fatal mistakes."

Robbie nodded. He remembered Shivers and their head-long descent.

"What are the Big Two?" Dad asked.

"Don't eat anything except blueberries, and if you see a moose, don't stay in the open. Get behind a tree."

"Right. And when you leave your backyard, there's a third. Don't get lost. There are things you have to do—"

"Like marking the way."

"Exactly. Make sure you always know where you are. If you get excited about going this direction or that—before you do, stop and look around. Which way did you come from? How will you find your way back? What will stick in your memory if you get confused? That's *your* job, no one else's. Whether you're with a friend or alone." He gave Robbie a searching look. "Got it?"

"Yep."

"You never know," Dad laughed. "You might want to come home."

Robbie grinned and settled back, and Dad began to read.

3

It rained for a week. Robbie was stuck inside with Mom, or with Trudy when Mom was gone. Through the back window, he watched the forest. Had Shivers claimed it? No, the trees weren't bothered by the damp and the fog. They grew quickly. Wherever branch ends met sky, there were sprays of leaves. Every day new bursts of green appeared on the Hill, till the aspen tops swayed beneath resplendent crowns. It was all happening without them.

Fristeen was never far from his thoughts. He fogged the glass with his breath and drew her running: a stick figure in the shrubs. And then she was there on the deck outside, waiting. It was nothing but wishing—just fog and mist. So he rubbed her away and started again. It all seemed impossible after what Mom had said.

When it was dark, he lay down, hoping for sun the next day. And when he got up, it was still raining and his vigil continued.

"Jim's coming over to play," Mom said one morning. "You like him."

Robbie nodded.

He met Jim in kindergarten, but they weren't really friends. Mom liked Jim's mom because she was smart and taught at the University. She brought some books for Mom, and the two women talked in the kitchen. Jim stood in the living room, checking things out.

He was holding something over his heart. It was shiny and red—a plastic car. He sat down on the floor and looked this way and that—the coast seemed clear. He bunched himself up, made a grumbling sound and sprang forward, driving his car around a chair.

Robbie stood and watched. Jim had an imagination, but it wasn't anything like his.

The car circled the sofa. Robbie followed along. Jim jumped on the cushions and drove over the top. Suddenly, from his throat came a gargling and crackling, and he raised his arm terribly and brought it down. His arm was a chain saw. It cut the sofa in two. He drove the car down the canyon, back onto the floor.

"I've been in the forest," Robbie said over the noise.

The car careened past him and circled the cordwood.

Robbie pointed through the window. "To the top of the Hill."

Jim nodded excitedly and the grumbling mounted.

"If it ever stops raining—"

"Watch me," Jim shouted. He drove his car up the window and along the spine of the Hill.

Robbie frowned. Mom was wrong—he didn't like Jim. And he was upset with himself. The forest was a secret. Jim descended the glass and zoomed toward the stove. Robbie turned from the race and headed for his room. *The forest,* he thought, *belongs to me and Fristeen.*

That evening, he was with her. "Sweet dreams," Dad said when he kissed him goodnight, and the place he drifted into when the light switched off couldn't have been sweeter. No rain, no Shivers, no Jim and no rules. Just a woodland wrung with yearning and Robbie in it, gazing up. Fristeen— Fristeen filled the sky, her smile like the sun, and no matter how much he drank of it, the warmth still poured down. Bedtime would never darken the spirit again. This new light had such energy that it could burn forever.

⁓

He woke the next morning feeling hollowed out, expecting the worst. But when he peered through the window, the sky was clear.

Mom left for work as soon as Trudy arrived. It didn't take Trudy long to get absorbed in her things. She filed her nails, she fussed with her curls, then she called one of her friends. She was facing the back door, so Robbie crept out the front.

Rules and promises— Dad understood. Some things you have to do, no matter what.

Not far from the edge of the Clearing, he found a crooked path. The shrubs were dripping, and before he had lost sight of the deck, his pants were soaked. He expected a house to burst into view, but the path kept twisting. It entered a tall thicket. Could he find it? What if he never saw her again?

Then the alders parted, and there it was. A house smaller than his own, but full in the sun. Someone had painted it yellow. Half of it, anyway. The other half was brown.

Was this where she lived?

Robbie stepped around to the front, patting his thighs, very excited.

A big motorcycle, silver and black, was parked on the gravel.

Who would answer the door? Fristeen? Probably not. He strode up to it, mustered his courage and raised his hand to knock. Then he stopped.

He could hear adult voices inside.

Robbie lowered his hand.

Suddenly the door swung open and a dark figure barged out. Large boots and grimy jeans swept beneath a shiny black coat. The man's cheeks were bearded and a swoop of black hair beetled over his brow. In the gap between, suspicious eyes darted.

"Liberty caps, Duane," a woman said from the doorway. "Don't forget."

The man nodded, folded some money and put it in his pocket. He almost knocked Robbie down.

"Hey, shorty. Watch out."

He laughed and straddled his cycle, coat squeaking like there were animals inside. Then his machine roared to life and the gravel was flying. Robbie turned, taking the stings on his back and shoulders.

As the clamor subsided, he realized the door was still ajar.

The woman stood watching him. She was beautiful, with long chestnut hair that fell in sleek waves, and deep blue eyes. She was wearing a robe, but it wasn't like Mom's.

"You must be Robbie."

He nodded. The robe was short and red, and sun was caught in its folds.

"I'm Grace," she said.

Robbie smiled hello.

Her brows twitched strangely. For a moment, he thought she was going to make fun of him. Then her features sobered and she motioned him closer. She had something in her hand—a baggie with dried-up plants inside.

"Would you like to come in?"

Robbie nodded.

Fristeen, he thought as he stepped through the door. Honey melting in tea—it was her smell. The living room was different than his. All the stuff was on the floor where you could reach it. A mattress, some pillows and blankets. Grace pointed at a cushion and Robbie sat down.

"Fristeen," Grace called. "Your friend is here."

A moment of silence, then a wild squeal. At the rear, Robbie saw a door pry open. Fristeen peeked out and ducked back.

"Just a minute," Grace said.

She disappeared and Robbie could hear them on the other side of the wall. Fristeen cried out and Grace made conciliating sounds. Then Fristeen was chattering. "No," she insisted, "like this." Grace made a disbelieving sound and Fristeen giggled. Still more yammering, and then the door opened and Grace stepped forward.

"The angel will be with us soon." She sat on the mattress opposite Robbie. "Well now. Finally." She folded her legs beneath her and regarded him with curiosity.

It wasn't unpleasant. Not like when a grownup inspects you. She had magical eyes, gentle and hesitant, and they drew you inside, just like Fristeen's. And once you were in there, it was all wonder and excitement and playful surprises.

"Not so fast, Romeo," Grace laughed. "I've heard about you."

Robbie laughed back.

Grace reached for something on the mattress. It was like a tiny box of kleenex. She pulled some tissues out and stuck them together. Then she opened the baggie and put some of the dried plants inside. She fooled with it, and it turned into a cigarette. She lit it and took a deep breath, peering through the smoke at him.

"I'm mystified." She exhaled in his direction. "Fristeen says—"

38

Robbie sniffed at the sweet vapor.

"—you're *very* close."

Robbie nodded. "I'm going to marry her."

Grace eyed him with amazement. "In one day?"

"Yep."

"It's so different—" She turned aside. "When you're older. When you sleep with the one you love."

"I'd like to do that."

Grace burst out laughing. "I'm sorry." She gave him a kindly look. "I'm sure it will be wonderful when you do."

Then something made her choke, her arms wrapped around her middle and she gave a piteous groan. "Oh—" Her eyes closed tightly and she rocked from side to side. "I have a Romeo, too. He'll find me, Robbie."

Her longing went through him like an electric shock.

"Someday." Grace gazed sadly at him.

Robbie saw the tears in her eyes. She drew on her cigarette again and unfolded her legs. Her robe parted, and he could see the inside of her thigh.

"Don't get any ideas." Grace gave him a reproving look and closed her robe. But she was just having fun. Her eyes sparkled like Fristeen's and they played the same game. The sparkle drew you in, then it moved and you lost it, and you had to find it again. That's the way women are, Robbie thought. The beautiful kind. They had little stars that played hide-and-seek with your mind.

"Are you Fristeen's mom?"

Grace made an odd face and nodded.

Robbie wondered what it would be like to have a mom like that.

"Here I am," Fristeen cried.

Robbie hopped to his feet.

The bedroom door swung open and Fristeen whirled out, a riot of color and flying things. Above the churning galaxy, her eyes flashed secret looks.

"Forgive us our fantasies," Grace said. "It's all we have."

The tornado whirled to a halt. Fristeen lowered her arms and they came to rest on her dress. It was emerald green, but it seemed to have burst. There were pieces cut out of it, and things attached. Swatches of fabric, pictures from magazines and books. Glued and pinned, or hanging loose on green yarn. Her hair was even crazier than before—a confusion of knots on top, with bows on either side.

Robbie swallowed. "I thought about you."

"Oh my," Grace murmured.

Fristeen smiled, but something made her hesitate.

"Give your prince a hug," Grace said. She reached out to catch a photo of a bird as it fell off its thread, but when she moved to re-tie it, Fristeen drew back. "We were up nights working on it," Grace told Robbie.

"It was my idea," Fristeen said stiffly, eyeing the cigarette.

Grace stood with the smoke coiling up from one hand, and the detached bird in the other.

"Would you like to go out?" Fristeen asked.

Robbie nodded uncertainly.

Fristeen clasped his hand and wheeled him away from her mother. When Robbie glanced back, Grace was smirking and shaking her head.

She followed them to the front door. "Where will you be?" Grace asked.

Fristeen gave her a long-suffering look.

"Don't mind me," Grace recanted. And then, "Robbie—"

He turned, hearing the suspense in her voice.

Grace's eyes glittered. "Set the woods on fire."

They hurried along the path away from the house.

"I like her," Robbie said.

Fristeen made a witless face.

"Does she make you brush your teeth?"

"She doesn't make me do anything."

"That man on the motorcycle—"

"Duane."

"Is he your dad?"

Fristeen looked irritated and shook her head. Some passing thought held her captive for a moment. "Dada doesn't live with us right now. Do you want to see our farm?"

"Sure."

She took a jog in the path. They threaded through low brush till they reached an unsettled place where the earth had been churned into hummocks. Fireweed was everywhere. In the middle was a tractor. It was rusted and caked with mud, and one of the tires was flat.

"We grow corn and melons—" Fristeen said. "All kinds of things."

They returned to the path and hurried along it, their excitement mounting as they started up the Hill.

"Go from tree to tree," Fristeen reminded him, "and don't stop between."

Everything had changed. The red currant fans sheltered broods of tiny blooms, and the bushes had gone crazy. All the buds had burst, and everywhere they turned there were bunches of leaves. And when the wind lifted, each was a galaxy flashing—they all did just what Fristeen had done with her dress.

High above, the aspen crowns seemed about to touch. Their leaves fluttered like the wings of invisible birds. You couldn't hear the sound indoors, but here beneath them it was really loud. No need to touch their trunks now, their thoughts were gushing: a million strange secrets all whispering at once, thrilling but soothing, like the sigh of the spout when you're filling the tub.

As they reached the top, the magic sound ceased. When they turned to look, the leaves were perfectly still. The wind had stopped, and across the slope, all the invisible birds had flown.

"It's like someone's watching," Fristeen said softly.

"Are you scared?" Robbie turned, scanning earth and sky.

"No sign of Shivers," Fristeen observed.

Robbie's brow crinkled. "Let's see what He Knows says."

They clasped hands, followed the Bendies and scrambled under the Fallen Down Trees. On the far bank of the stream bed, He Knows was waiting, looking grizzled and damp, squinting and glaring over his ragged goatee.

Robbie stepped forward. "Is it a good day to explore?"

"Warm, warm . . ."

Fristeen nodded. "The sun's going to shine."

"Hide, hide, hide, hide . . ."

That bothered Robbie.

"I like to hide," Fristeen shrugged.

"If something bad's going to happen, you better say so."

"No, no, no, no . . ."

"See," Fristeen laughed. "Relax."

"Pass, pass, pass, pass . . ."

So they continued along the bank, scooted over the log bridge and climbed the incline, pausing by the gate of stumps at the start of Where You Can See.

The way was clear and there was hardly a breeze.

Robbie stepped onto the ridge, feeling brave. There wasn't any reason to be afraid. "Come on," he motioned, and Fristeen caught up with him. They stood together, looking down on either side. There were more trees than you can imagine, and not a branch was bare now. It was an ocean of leaves.

"If we jumped, do you think they'd catch us?"

Robbie glanced at her and they both laughed.

They hurried up the crestline, passed the place they'd stopped at the week before, reached the high point of the ridge and then continued along it, descending. A confusion of hills and valleys opened before them.

"Nobody's ever been here before," Robbie said, recalling Fristeen's words.

She smiled. "We're the first."

Which way now? He pointed to the left. A slope was covered thickly with little trees. They started down. You had to hold on, and you kept slipping, but it wasn't that hard. The branches were covered with tiny white dots, and the leaves were sticky. Fristeen started singing, "Dot Trees, Dot Trees."

Robbie laughed. Long droopy things hung from the leaf clusters, covered with golden dust. "Shake them, shake them."

So they shook the branches, and the air sparkled as they descended. The Dot Trees were merry and liked that very much.

At the bottom of the slope, they came out onto a small meadow.

"What's wrong?" Fristeen asked.

"I'm thinking," Robbie said, turning.

"About what?"

"Getting lost." He eyed Fristeen's hair. Her bows were too small to see through the leaves. "Maybe—" He ran his hands through the paper and fabric adorning her dress.

Then he noticed: he was wearing white socks. He sat down, removed a shoe, and took one off. He tied it to a Dot Tree so it was in clear view.

"Perfect," she exclaimed, turning to embrace the meadow before them. "It's the Perfect Place."

44

Robbie regarded her. "It's perfect because you're here."

Fristeen glowed. They held hands and crossed the lush flat.

At its edge, wands rose from the soil, crankled and thin. They were heading right through them when Fristeen cried out.

"They're covered with needles."

Robbie yelped as one jabbed his leg.

He could see now—every wand was bristling—so they backed out and scouted along the edge of the patch. The plants grew thickly, there were impossible tangles, but Robbie found a place where a shadowy tunnel seemed to go through.

He dropped to all fours and wriggled forward. Fristeen followed close behind. The tunnel turned and dipped and rose toward the light. A stray needle stuck Robbie and he sucked his breath. Then his elbows emerged and he scrambled out.

"Made it." He gave her a victory grin. "Some of your things came off." He eyed her dress.

"It scratched you." Fristeen touched the scarlet squiggle on his arm.

"Yep."

She bent her head and kissed it.

Robbie reached out and stroked her hair. When he gazed into her eyes, they deepened and the stars didn't shift. No hide-and-seek now—no laughter, no fear. Just hope, and hurts that must be shared. The one you yearned for was here, and she yearned just like you did. Joy made love smile, but pain made it pure.

"Look—" Fristeen turned her head up.

Robbie peered into the sun.

"White," she said.

"Yep." It blasted your eyes.

"Now close," Fristeen said.

"Red," Robbie announced.

"And white," Fristeen flared her lids. "And red," closing again. "And white and red, and white and red—"

"And white and red—" Robbie joined in.

Faster and faster, open and close—your head was full of flashes, a pot boiling over. And then it did, and you fell down, clutching blindly for the other, euphoric and giggling.

Before they left, Robbie removed his other sock and marked the spot.

From there, a ledge stretched on the level, awned with thin aspens. They hurried along it, leaves Jiggling above. A breeze cooled them and pleased them, and then they reached water—not a lot, just a Trickle—and they hopped across.

Something rasped in their ears.

Robbie scanned the trees. A squirrel was scampering along a branch. When it reached the end, it rasped again.

"What do you want?" Robbie asked.

The squirrel just stared.

"Is it Shivers?" Fristeen wondered.

The squirrel wiggled its nose.

Robbie shook his head. "He's talking to us."

The squirrel twitched its tail, shrilled and made a chucking sound.

"What did he say?" Fristeen laughed.

The squirrel sprang from its perch into an alder nearby and went vaulting through the leaves.

"'Follow me,'" Robbie cried, and went racing after him.

The pursuit led them splashing through Trickle. The water kinked and raveled, and then suddenly it vanished and the ground dropped before them. They were on the rim of a bowl surrounded by low willows. On the branch of one, the squirrel sat, gazing down. The bowl was full of leaves.

"It's a secret place," Robbie said.

Overhead, a lattice had been woven by the trees' pale arms, and at every joint catkins were bursting, like a web of cracked pipes spraying liquid sun.

"What's that, over there?" Fristeen pointed.

Through the tangle of boughs, a hundred yards distant, dark islands seemed to drift. The trees on them were spiky and black, and each grew to a point. And there was space in between them, as if profusion was banned there, or some scourge had struck.

The squirrel chattered, calling their attention back.

"It's where you hide," Robbie said, remembering the words of He Knows.

"How far down does it go?"

Robbie dropped to his hands and knees. "Let's see." He started to descend.

Before long, he was thigh-deep in twigs and leaves. "It's crunchy on top," he tossed the litter in the air, "but it's soft beneath." Then he kicked up his feet and slid to the low point. "Come on," he cried.

47

Fristeen skied on her bottom to join him. Robbie pushed the leaves aside to make a space, and once they'd bedded in, he covered them over.

"It's warm," Fristeen giggled, squirming against him.

"Sh-h-h. We can't make any noise."

She bit her lips to seal them. Robbie caught his breath. Her red lips, and the white teeth pressed deeply— The sight set something churning inside him. "The Hiding Hole," he whispered.

"Nobody knows," Fristeen said.

"We can do whatever we want." He looked into her eyes.

"What should we do?"

Out of nowhere it came to him. "Count your teeth."

"Alright," she consented.

"Lay back."

She did as he said.

"Now open your mouth."

Her jaw parted and her teeth appeared.

"Okay. Here I go."

He began to count, using his forefinger to touch each one. They were hard and gleaming, with strange pits and points. They were all fascinating, but when he reached the first molar, other sights distracted him. The insides of her cheeks were silky and smooth, and led back to a cavern that descended into darkness. You could roll a marble down there, like the one he lost down the bathroom sink. Her tongue lay limp, like a little pillow, but when he touched it, it twitched and curled around his finger. That gave him a jolt.

48

"How many?" Fristeen wondered.

Robbie blinked. "I forget."

"Crazy boy." She poked his belly.

He laughed, pinched her nose and slid back beside her.

"Can you really fly?" Fristeen raised her finger and drew a trail through the clouds.

"In my dreams," Robbie said.

"Will you show me how?"

"Sure. It's easy to glide and turn," he explained. "And if you want to come down, you coast. Getting *up* there—that's the hard part. You have to catch the wind just right."

"You need wings—" She made a skeptical face.

Robbie shook his head. "Arms work fine."

She laughed. "I'm going to kiss you again." She raised herself, shook the leaves from her hair, and was halfway to his cheek when his expression stopped her.

"Fristeen—"

She waited for him to speak.

"Let's sleep together," Robbie said.

"Here?"

He nodded.

She thought for a moment. "Okay."

A coarse rasp sounded above them. The squirrel was hunched in the willow lattice, watching, and as they spotted him, he launched through the branches, chattering for all he was worth.

"He'll tell everyone," Fristeen warned, then she curled next to Robbie with her cheek on his shoulder. "That's nice."

49

Strands of her hair webbed his face. He could feel her breath.

"Did you ever have a girl for a friend?" she asked.

"No," he said. "Did you—"

She put her hand on his chest. "You're the first."

Robbie could feel her warmth all down his side, and then her lips pressed against his cheek. His hands were trembling. He had a presentiment, a feeling of anticipation unlike anything he'd experienced. Something really important was happening, but he wasn't sure what. "When you love someone, and you're sleeping with them—" He could barely speak. "You put your arms around them."

"You do other things, too."

"Yep." Robbie took a breath. "You kiss their lips."

"They're here," Fristeen said.

"Who?"

"Listen," Fristeen whispered.

Robbie listened, but he couldn't hear anything.

"Mister Squirrel and his friends." She lifted her shoulders and gazed around the Hole, pointing at different places on the rim. "Mousies and weasels— And nosy Miss Fox." She squealed, scooped some leaves up and hurled them at the lattice.

"What do they want?"

"We're the show," she fretted. "They've come to watch."

Through the falling leaves, Robbie saw them—snouts probing the lattice, whiskers twitching, beady eyes eager to see.

They settled on branches, crouching, hanging, chins sunk in crutches, teeth bared and grinning. Word had traveled fast.

"What should we do?"

"Don't let them." Fristeen shook her head. "They'll have all kinds of bad thoughts. Don't let them see *anything*."

"Get down," Robbie said. He grabbed her and drew her back beside him. Then he used both arms to sweep the leaves over them.

"That's good," she said, and she swept leaves too.

"Sh-sh-sh—" Robbie stopped her and turned his ear to listen.

The forest was suddenly quiet. Not a creature peeped.

"I'm scared," Fristeen whispered.

Robbie rustled his arms around her middle. She did the same, and they pressed each other close. His heart rose and he put his lips to hers.

"Oo oo oo," said the wild things. "Ah-hh-hh-hh."

Robbie glanced up. They were craning forward, bobbing their snouts. There was clicking and grunting, then heads turned as they conferred.

"See?" Fristeen whimpered. She pulled him back down and continued heaping leaves, covering their heads, burying them completely.

"It's okay."

She was clasping him desperately, chest heaving. When he touched her cheek, he could feel her tears.

"They think I'm like Grace."

"We're hiding." He stroked her temple. "It's okay."

"Dream boy—" She barely got the words out. Her tears came in a flood.

They lay in each other's arms for a long time. The animals grew bored. A couple of them spit insults at the squirrel.

Gradually, peace grew around them like a soft cocoon.

On the rim above, branches clacked in the wind. Or was it the sound of the beasts departing? Their fur was sleek and the sun in the west flashed on their backs. One hitched its whistle to a flying breeze. That was the last thing Robbie heard. Or had he already dozed off?

In a gray limbo, midway between asleep and awake, backlit clouds rotated in the gathering darkness. Where he lay, day was ending. It was damp and dreary, and the gloom was encroaching. But there, in that distant place, something promised awaited him. A great exultation. A dream like no other. The clouds were dissolving now, rays of fierce light speared through—glints of an eye, giant, all-seeing. A fierce flowering of the energy he felt with Fristeen. And Dad's great understanding, magnified a thousand times. Magic of magics, secret of secrets. Fearfully strange, but familiar, too. Like a memory rising from deep within you. Or an invisible companion, finally spied.

"Not that it matters," a deep voice murmured. "When you dream, there's no outside or in. Your mind is an unimaginable bloom. A willow catkin as big as the moon. With billions of anthers, shaking pollen like stars. It may seem strange, but in this boundless place— You're not alone.

"I've been watching. I know what you want and who you are.

"Your home is a prison. Your mother's a drone. Those wild seeds of your father's will never get sown. Fate sent you Fristeen, and you like to explore. 'The cosmos,' Dad says. Baby steps, Robbie. Baby steps—nothing more.

"When your baby teeth are gone, who will you be?

"One who waits to be eaten? Food for despair? Or one who broke free?

"Look into my eye. I'm your dreams reaching out. The Fristeen you yearn for, that thrill, that ache— When you're full to the brim with her? That's just a taste. I'm here. I'm waiting. But I'll be moving on soon.

"This time is yours—summer's ahead. Until the trees yellow, the dreams are on me. No thoughts of leaving. Not yet. Just feel free. Dream, Robbie. Dream. What shall it be? A pram up Raging River to where day and night meet? A cable-ride in a basket between Venus and Mars? A flight through the heart of an exploding star? You and Fristeen— Take every chance, awake or asleep. Find the door, spring the hatch, pry the gap between sill and sash.

"Dream, Robbie, dream. Right here, right now. Anything you choose. Crack the sun open and paint your face with its yolk. Cast the fragments from you and turn the world to smoke. Pull the tacks from the night and roll the sky up. A new universe? Say the word—I'll make one for you. You, just you and little Fristeen. I'm the Dream Man. Bid your curled body goodbye, and come with me."

4

They woke to a gray sky. Fearful the weather might turn, they hurried back. It was harder to see the needles, and they got badly pricked. By the time they reached He Knows, the cloud cover was like a finger painting, all dark knots and windings. They parted at the bottom of the Hill. Robbie felt Fristeen's presence even after she'd disappeared down the path.

Then he was standing there, facing the back door, alone.

Trudy will be furious, he thought.

Sure enough. She was on the sofa, and when he stepped across the threshold, she closed her pocket mirror with a snap. "You brat—" She lunged and got hold of him.

He went limp, slipping through her hands onto the floor.

"Bear, bear—" He rocked with delirium.

"You'll wish one had," she sneered, looming over him.

Robbie sighed and raised himself.

"First, you'll scrub out the tub. Then you can paint my toe-nails. Just wait, wonderboy. You'll be locked up all summer."

She was right, Robbie knew. Mom would be merciless. He ground his teeth and headed for his room.

Then he felt Trudy's hand on his shoulder.

When he looked back, she was scowling. Under the mop of red curls, he could see the white flag in her eyes.

They sat at the dining room table and talked things over. It would be better, Trudy said, if Mom and Dad didn't find out. Robbie agreed. He promised not to tell where he had gone, and she promised to keep his absence a secret. Trudy called on Jesus as a witness and they shook hands. Then she fixed him a sandwich.

He ate in silence, examining the living room as he chewed. The stove was there, and the woodpile beside it. The reading chair. The glass-top table. He stood and circled the room, still chewing, wondering what had changed. On the mantle was the picture of Mom by Old Faithful, the flower of glass beads that Grandma made, the rocks Dad found who knows where. Robbie felt like a stranger.

He wandered down the hall, peering into his room and Mom and Dad's. Trudy was in front of their dresser putting away laundry. It was all familiar, but the house seemed different. It was stark and vacant, as if the people who lived there had just moved in. *They won't be staying long*, Robbie thought. He laughed. Where did that idea come from?

The pact with Trudy opened the way. Mom was gone three days a week, and on those days, Robbie did as he pleased. He made Fristeen promise not to come to his house, but he didn't tell her why. Sometimes she waited in the shrubs for him. Other times he found her at home.

It was always exciting when Grace was around. She'd say things that surprised you, or do things you didn't think grownups would do. She liked seeing him, even early in the morning, and she didn't fuss if she wasn't dressed. She'd bend over and he'd see her bottom, or her robe would fall open and he'd see her breasts. They were hard and pointy, not round and squishy like Mom's. And what was best—she didn't have rules. She never intruded—Fristeen made sure of that.

Often Grace was gone and they had the house to themselves. They both liked to draw. They'd tear open a grocery bag and spread it out on the floor.

"An eye?" Fristeen guessed.

Robbie nodded. It was all he remembered of him. The stranger hadn't come again. "Something I dreamed."

There was a puzzle of a princess Fristeen was working on. They pieced her face together. Then they filled in the sunrise behind her, and the baby in the crystal ball. Sometimes Robbie brought his marbles, or his bow and arrows. They'd play inside till the time felt right to turn their minds to more serious things. Then eyes would meet and a daring look would flash, and they'd be out the door, beating toward the forest.

57

They might forge a new path and do real exploring. Or visit familiar places—there was always something to see. Every day that passed, the branches reached farther and the leaves grew thicker. The perfect weather seemed like it would never end. Shivers? There was no trace of him—maybe he'd vanished for good. One day they rolled onto their backs beneath the Jigglies, and Robbie gazed up and hissed through his teeth.

"What are you doing?" Fristeen giggled.

Robbie kicked his feet. "Making them grow."

"You can't do that—"

He hissed again and pointed excitedly. The sun was blinding, the wind up there steady—the high tips of the Jigglies were going wild.

"They're not—" Fristeen began.

"Look," Robbie cried.

She gasped in amazement—he was right. The branches grew longer as she watched. Leaves were shooting out like water from a hose.

A cloud covered the sun one afternoon, and Robbie feared Shivers might be stalking them. But Fristeen knew better. She raised her arms, touched the hot gold with both hands, and gave a great push. And the sun rose from its nest into clear sky.

"Have you ever had a secret friend?" Fristeen wondered.

"Just you," Robbie said.

"I'm not really secret." She gave him a mysterious smile.

There was one place that sobered them, no matter how cheery they were. When they faced the Needle Patch, they knew the price they would pay to pass. Flowers sprang from the Perfect Place as if to prepare them, green stalks bearing up little white crowns; and as you stepped through them, a sweet resin filled the air. The Patch was waiting, in a deceptive guise. It had bright leaves now, and among them, chalice-shaped blooms—pink with lemon centers—but the needles were still there. They were just harder to see.

When they found the tunnel, they would kneel down. There was no need for words—it was a trial they would share. Robbie went first, making himself as small as he could, and they shirked and cringed as the tunnel kinked. But before they emerged, the Patch had done what it wanted, and one—often both—had blood-colored scrawls penned on their skin.

One morning, there was something in the tunnel with them. It was right in front of him, but Robbie didn't see it till it sprang from the leaves. A blur of speckled feathers, brown and brick, whirred through the hedge—the shock pricked them both. They clutched their wounds, hearing its trailing whimper as the grouse beat away through the trees.

They only returned once to the Hiding Hole, and they didn't go down. There wasn't any reason to hide. They held hands whenever they felt like it, and sometimes they'd hug and kiss when the animals weren't around. There weren't bathrooms in the forest, and that embarrassed them at first. "I have to go. Don't peek—" But the frequent calls of nature put an end to giggles, and when a private moment was needed, it was taken without fuss.

Old places or new, Robbie marked the way. Socks, his and Dad's, and some of Mom's dust rags. As the forest leafed out, they were harder to find. He'd move them, and he'd have to move them again. Look back, look forward, check the way between.

Mom never suspected. She would return from work and ask what he'd done, and he would say something stupid like, "I collected leaves," or "Nothing," and she was happy as can be.

Aunt Verna sent him a present, and they called to thank her.

"He's nearly four feet tall," Mom said.

"They'd fit Uncle Abe," Aunt Verna laughed.

When Mom hung up, she put the gift back in the box. Robbie stopped her.

"You've never liked red socks."

"Oh no, Mom." He grabbed them. "These are great."

One day, Mom came home in an especially good mood.

"I've got the next two weeks off," she told Robbie. "No Trudy," she hugged him. "Just you and me."

That meant trouble. Whenever he opened the door, Mom would go out with him. He could play in the Clearing or walk up the Hill. But she was at the window or on the deck constantly, watching. He didn't dare venture beyond the Hill's top, or through the shrubs in the direction of Fristeen's house.

When Mom was in the kitchen, he'd shuffle into the living room and stare at the phone. Robbie had made calls before, but he'd always had help. He thought he could do it, but he needed Fristeen's number and hadn't a clue how to get it. The weather was fine. She must have been wondering. He hoped she wouldn't come looking. But that's what she did.

It was early in the morning. Robbie was at the table, eating cereal with Mom. Dad had finished and was gathering his books in the den. There was a knock at the back door. Mom turned her head, puzzled. Then she stood, crossed the living room, and peered through the window. Robbie sat perfectly still.

Mom opened the door. "Yes?"

"Is Robbie here?" Fristeen asked.

Behind Mom's dark outline, Robbie saw a turquoise skirt shift. Fristeen peeked in, saw him and waved.

Then Mom stepped outside and pulled the door shut.

Robbie listened. He couldn't hear anything but the thumping in his chest. Dad was returning from the den with his daypack, ready to leave for the University. He knelt, put an arm around Robbie and kissed his temple.

"Where's Mom?"

The back door opened.

"Jack—"

Robbie's heart sank.

"We had a visitor." Mom gestured at the door. "Take a guess."

Dad gave her a mystified look.

"Her name is Fristeen." Mom glared at Robbie.

Dad shook his head and stood. He turned to leave.

"Jack? Goddammit— We have to talk about this."

Robbie slid out of his chair. He was headed for his room, but as Dad faced Mom, he ran and stood beside him. Dad cupped his shoulder.

"Is she still out there?" Dad asked.

"No. I sent her home."

"Well?"

"They're pals. They've been playing together." Mom stared at Robbie. "He goes to her house all the time."

Dad took a breath and put his pack down. Robbie gazed up at him. Dad stroked his hair. "So fucking what," Dad said.

Mom's ire shattered. "There's no telling what goes on in that house. That biker's done time. I saw her at the grocery last week. She was lost—pupils big as quarters. They had to drive her home."

Dad looked out the window. Had something caught his eye? He slid one hand into his pocket, his brow twitching imperceptibly. Sometimes Robbie imagined he could hear what Dad was thinking. But not now.

"I've seen that little girl," Mom said, "wandering around by herself a mile from here. The woman isn't responsible enough to have a child."

Dad nodded. "Well—fine." He looked at Robbie. "Your mom's—" The corner of his mouth hooked. "You know the rules."

"Dad—" Robbie heard himself sniveling. The sound shamed him. Was he going to cry?

"Don't hide behind your father," Mom warned him. "There's going to be a punishment for all of this."

"Felicia—"

"Robbie, go to your room." Mom jerked him free of Dad.

"It's not as bad as—"

"It's worse," Mom said.

Robbie shuffled away, entered his room and closed the door behind him. Then he put his ear to it.

"He's been lying to us. He's been wandering all over these woods with that little girl."

"Happy to hear it."

Robbie's spirit soared. Dad wasn't giving in.

"He's going too far," Mom said.

"What? Doing things he's never done?"

"He doesn't have the judgment—"

"And he won't need any with you off work. You can choose his friends for him, decide where he should go and what he should do—" Dad was angry. Really angry. "I don't blame him for lying. I'd act the same—"

"I can't do this alone, Jack. I can't do it!"

"You're losing it."

"We should never have had a child together," Mom said.

Robbie had a sick feeling in his center. What made her say that? He listened for Dad's response, but the silence stretched out.

"Maybe not," Dad said.

63

"You're not ready to be a father."

"And you're every boy's nightmare. Can't you understand—he wants some freedom."

"*He's six years old,*" Mom screamed. Then she began to sob.

The little house's warmth shrank into the corners. Robbie shivered. Why did this have to happen? They hadn't been arguing as much. Things were getting better.

"Do you know how hard it is for me to be the bad guy?" Mom said through her tears. She was giving in.

Robbie hoped Dad was hugging her.

"What's happened to you?" Dad said. "Is this the same woman who walked the Pinnacles with me at midnight? He needs to wander. When I was his age—"

"—in Illinois—"

"Yes, Illinois." Dad's voice deepened. "The girl from the Upper West Side thought having a forest for your backyard was pretty cool. 'Daniel Boone.'"

"Please, Jack—"

"Daniel got lost. He fell and cut his head open. The river ice gave way beneath him and he nearly drowned. But he survived. I'm sorry if I keep replaying all of this for you, but it defined me— I learned to trust my instincts, to take risks and face danger. I fell in love with wild things—"

"The perfect childhood," Mom said acidly.

"It was rotten," Dad replied. "But on this point, they were wise."

"They were oblivious," Mom sighed. "They were gambling with your life. And there weren't any bears. Daniel's friends killed them all." She sniffed back her tears. "You didn't mean it, did you? You're not sorry we—"

"Of course not."

"So much has changed. We were so naive about this Ph.D. program."

"Stop worrying."

"I can't. I see the account shrinking every month. I don't mind working, but Robbie—"

"You need to get out of the house, and stay out of his way. I'm not going through another winter like the last one."

Robbie held his breath. This was a bad subject.

"The storms drove me crazy," Mom flared.

"You wouldn't get out of bed."

"That's what you do when it's dark! And it's dark *all the time*. Maybe we should face up to it. Alaska, the whole thing—"

"Can this wait?"

Dad was finished. He was going to leave.

"What are we going to do about—"

"Nothing," Dad said. "Robbie's fine. Let him roam to his heart's content."

"And the girl?"

"Come on, Felicia. You think Robbie's getting high with her?"

"No, but—"

"But what?"

"Talk to him about honesty. Please. Do that for him, will you? He needs to be honest with us. I want to trust him."

The conversation faded and Robbie retreated to his toy box. When Dad walked through the door, he was sitting on the floor, spinning a top.

When he glanced up, he was surprised at Dad's expression. Dad looked glum, not like he usually did after he'd won an argument.

Dad sat down on the bed.

Robbie waited for him to speak, but he just stared at the brain poster with an absent look.

"Dad?"

"Mmm?"

"Are you okay?"

Dad traced a line on his palm with his forefinger.

"Should we talk? Robbie asked.

"I guess so."

Robbie waited, but Dad remained mute.

"What should we talk about?" Robbie said, sitting beside him.

Dad took a breath.

"Should we talk about honesty?" Robbie wondered.

Dad was motionless for a long moment. Then he lifted his face, regarded him knowingly and shook his head. "Goodbye." He kissed Robbie on the temple, rose, and walked out.

5

After Dad left, Robbie ventured out of his room.

Mom was in the kitchen, cleaning up.

"Is everything okay?"

She nodded and smiled. "What would you like to do today?" She acted as if nothing had happened.

"Play out back."

"Your dad and I agree—you can go beyond the top of the Hill."

"What about—"

"That's alright, too." Mom turned away from him to put some dishes in the cupboard. "You can play with Fristeen. But I would be happier if you were here or in the forest. Let's not be spending a lot of time at her house." She faced him.

Robbie hugged her. "You're a great mom."

She knelt and kissed him, seeing the anxiety in his eyes.

"There's a beacon inside you," Mom whispered. "Your best guide through life." She held him tightly. "Don't worry about a thing." After a long moment, she drew back, wiped the corner of his mouth and kissed his cheek. "You haven't had any trouble finding your way? No moose or bears?"

Robbie shook his head.

"You've met Fristeen's mother?"

Robbie nodded.

Mom seemed about to say something. But she decided not to. "Alright then. Be careful."

Robbie nodded and hugged her one last time. Then he headed for the back door.

When he knocked, Fristeen's face appeared in the gap. She looked surprised, then her eyes beamed gratitude and the door swung open.

"You came." She stepped forward to embrace him, and the sun spilled over them.

"I'm sorry," Robbie said, thinking of the days he'd missed her.

"Your mom doesn't like me."

Robbie saw how fearful she was. "Something's wrong with my mom," he said. "Dad wants her to see the doctor."

"Is she sick?"

"Sort of," Robbie nodded. He turned toward the forest. "Let's go."

"Wait." Fristeen ducked inside. She returned with something wrapped in a hanky.

"What's that?"

"A snack. Put it in your pocket."

"Thanks, Grace," Robbie shouted.

Fristeen shook her head. "She isn't here."

Robbie grabbed her hand and they headed for the path.

It was a glorious day, like He Knows predicted. All the leaves had grown larger and the crowns were thick. They raced up Where You Can See, stopped at the high point, joined hands and whirled around. The forest tilted and pivoted, and they flung their heads back and stretched their arms, whirling faster and faster, until it seemed that everything in sight was flying away from them, disappearing over the rim of the world. Then they lowered themselves through the Dot Trees, and ran out onto the Perfect Place.

"Robbie— Look." Fristeen fell to her knees beside a plant with purple bell flowers hanging in clusters from a leafy top. They were everywhere, woven among the white crowns, and when she turned the bells up, there were little suns inside.

"Smell," Robbie said. Balsam rose from the meadow like smoke from a lamp.

Fristeen shut her eyes. "One, two," she counted as she sniffed, "three, four. Smell four times."

Robbie followed her example. When he opened his eyes, hers were very close.

"I love Grace," Fristeen said. "But I love you more."

Robbie thought about his parents. He loved them both, but only Dad understood— Fristeen drew him back with a fervent look.

"I'm going to leave Grace," she said, "and be with you."

"That would be great. But Mom wouldn't let you."

Fristeen shook her head. "Here, in the forest. With the trees and the sun." She tipped her face up.

Could they do that? Robbie wondered.

Her eyes narrowed to slits, feeling the sun's caress. "She misses us when we're gone," Fristeen said softly. "She pretends we're with her."

She raised one brow at him. "No more brushing teeth."

Robbie laughed.

"Let's have our treat." Fristeen pointed, and Robbie drew the surprise from his pocket. There was a brownie inside and she broke it in half.

Robbie looked around as he chewed. "This would be a good spot—" He put his finger in his mouth. "There are crunchy things."

Fristeen giggled. "Those are seeds, silly. A good spot for what?"

"To have our home."

The idea welled up between them and flooded the Perfect Place. For a long moment, their minds bobbed on it, and all of the blooms were floating.

Robbie brought them back. "Are you ready?"

Fristeen pursed her lips.

They stood together and stepped toward the Needle Patch. At the entrance to the tunnel, he knelt and they squirmed inside.

They emerged, nursed their wounds, and passed beneath the Jigglies lost in their separate thoughts. But when they reached Trickle, they shared them. As so often happened, they had been thinking the same thing: today was the day to strike a new path.

"Want to see what's *there*?" Robbie pointed.

Just beyond Trickle, the ground rose. Fristeen nodded and approached the slope. It was covered with thick scrub. Nothing could be seen through the looming tangle.

Robbie pulled a rag from his pocket and found a place to tie it. Then they started up.

The boughs were rubbery and reluctant. You had to talk firmly to them and hold them apart. They didn't want you to see what was ahead. And when the last of them gave in and put their arms down, Robbie and Fristeen understood why. A grove of giant trees rose before them—taller, much taller than you thought trees could be.

"They're the tallest ones in the world," Fristeen said.

"Sh-sh-sh." Robbie put his finger to his lips.

They approached them slowly, and then they were among them, gazing up. The crowns were so high, they were like green clouds. There were leaves and they were moving—you could see them way up there, winking shadows and light. No small trees grew between the giants, just little ferns. Their shoes went *crunch-crunch* on the dead leaves.

"What's that?" Fristeen whispered.

Robbie heard it too. Something was rustling beneath the carpet. But you couldn't tell where. It was like a story Dad was reading—you were lost in it, but you could hear his fingers turning the pages.

Right at their feet, two little birds sprang free.

Fristeen jumped and clutched Robbie, and then they were laughing. But not loudly, just to each other.

"I feel tiny," Fristeen said as they continued. Most of the giants were white, but here was a silver one, and there was a copper one. And through the columns ahead, one was pink. Gradually their confidence mounted. They drew deeper breaths and stood a little straighter. They were walking in step.

"They're great," Robbie said, feeling the solemnity of the grove inside him.

"Great," Fristeen murmured.

They were the Great trees, and this was the Great Place.

At the rear of the grove was a tree unlike the rest. It was short and huddled, and its bark was dark. Its branches hung down, some to the ground. You could crawl inside, and that's what they did.

"A tent," Robbie said, looking around.

"Let's sit."

They sat with their backs against the thick trunk.

"It's the Safe Tree," Fristeen said. "You can't worry about anything here. The Safe Tree won't let you."

Robbie gave it a try. He thought about what they might encounter beyond the Great Place—a moose, or Shivers. And Fristeen was right the thoughts just flew away. They were under the Safe Tree and everything was okay. He felt for her hand and they shared the safe silence.

"Want to know a secret?" Fristeen asked.

"Sure."

"I talk to you before I go to sleep. Every night."

"Wow."

"I'm just laying there . . . feeling that special way . . ." She squeezed his hand. "I pretend there's nobody in the whole world but you and me, and . . . my other friend."

"Your other friend?"

"My stuffed bear," she said. "I tell you how happy I am— And then I don't say anything at all. That's the strange part. You *know*. You hear what I'm thinking, and you know just how I feel . . ." Her voice trailed off.

Safety filtered through the shade.

"I've got a secret, too," Robbie said.

"What?"

"I wasn't brave before."

"Oh—" She gave a dismissing huff.

"No, really. Things always scared me." He thought about

73

that. "They still scare me, I guess. But I do them anyway. I'm brave because of you."

She saw the deep feeling in his eyes and kissed his lips.

"Let's do it now," Robbie said.

Fristeen made a confused face.

"You know—" Robbie touched her hand. "What we talked about."

Fristeen looked down.

He didn't want to embarrass her, so he whispered in her ear.

"You—" She shoved his shoulder.

"I'm not afraid," he said.

"Yes you are."

"I'm not," he laughed. He stood on his knees and fumbled for his zipper.

Fristeen shrieked.

Robbie couldn't get his pants undone. His hands were trembling.

"Don't," Fristeen cried.

The cloth parted.

"Stop, stop—" She was hiding her face.

Robbie closed his eyes and pulled his pants down. "Can you see?"

"Take your hand away, silly."

Robbie held his breath. "Well?" He let a little light between his lids.

Fristeen was staring, stunned.

He felt instantly self-conscious. "What's wrong?" he said, pulling his pants up.

She was still staring. "He moved."

Robbie shrugged and knelt before her.

Fristeen shook her head. "Does he do what you say?"

"Sure," Robbie said. "He's not like us."

That made her laugh. Robbie laughed too. They laughed until they calmed down.

"Now you," he said.

Fristeen stared at him for a long moment. Then she reached under her dress.

Robbie stooped. It was hard to see in the dim tent. "A little pocket," he whispered.

Fristeen nodded. Then she drew her panties up and looked away.

Robbie waited. Her breathing was long and deep.

"I want to leave," she said.

They crawled out of the Safe Tree and stood in the sun at the edge of the Great Place.

Robbie faced her, but neither spoke.

"Can we hug?" he asked.

She didn't reply. He could see the anguish in her eyes.

Robbie swallowed. "What's wrong? Did I—" It was like a stroke of bright watercolor on a wet page. Doubt bled in all directions.

Fristeen made an angry face. "We aren't married."

Robbie's heart rose. "I love you," he said, reaching out.

Her distress burst like a bubble and she fell forward, limp and gasping.

Robbie held her close. "Nothing's changed."

Fristeen clung to him, unable to speak.

He stood there, rocking her gently. *It was brave to have said that,* he thought. I love you— A vast unknown had opened between them, and he'd crossed it with a single breath.

After a while, Fristeen's self-possession returned. When she was ready, they turned their backs on the Great grove and started through the high brush, climbing. She didn't say anything, but Robbie had never felt so close to her. Maybe the revelations beneath the Safe Tree *had* changed them. They moved with a new fluency, holding the boughs back for each other, one in the lead and then the other, as if testing a deeper trust.

The web loosened. The litter shimmied, fooling their feet. Then the way leveled, and they stepped through jade-leaved willows bursting with wool. They came upon a log that was rotting. Its thick trunk lay intact on the soil, but its arms were gone and its bark was blanketed with dogwood crosses. "It's not a tree," Robbie said. "But it used to be." So that's what they called it.

They headed to the left, and as Used-to-Be disappeared behind and below them, a ridge rose up. On the crest, a pair of aspens were silhouetted against the sky. As they approached, Robbie could see that the aspens were wrapped around each other. He glanced back. The view spread out: a choppy descent, a line of hills lifting up, and a river of leaves flowing between—trees beyond counting, every shade of green.

When they reached the top, there were a couple of surprises. The two aspens had sprung from the same mass of roots.

"Like us, " Fristeen said.

"The Two-Tree." Robbie put his fingers in the crevice between the boles. And then he froze. A ghostly landscape met their eyes—shot with bright colors, but ravaged and gloomy—No crowns or green canopies. The trees were all black—spindly and pointed, as far as you could see. Robbie remembered the islands they'd glimpsed from the Hiding Hole's rim.

"Where are we?" Fristeen drew closer.

He gave her a mystified look. He scanned the decline and pointed. The border of the dark domain was just below. Should they go see?

A silent "dare you" passed between them. They nodded to each other, linked hands, and started down.

The way descended through thick viburnum, a puzzle of leaves that obscured the way forward at every step. A sudden break—the black trees were closer—then they vanished again behind the shifting green.

"Look," Fristeen cried out.

Ahead, the ground was splashed with color—emerald, russet, maroon and rose. She ran and knelt down in it. Robbie followed, amazed by the swells on either side. It was moss, but not like any he'd ever seen. It spread out like a giant quilt, covering everything. When you put your foot down, you sank way in.

Fristeen screeched. She was hopping and sloshing from swell to swell. Robbie leaped after her. The moss bled, and the blood smelled like Christmas. Your feet got soaked. You sank deeper and deeper—up to your knees—but it wasn't hard to get out. More wild colors—amber and mauve, burnt lake and chartreuse—and all so bright, magically bright. There was a little wet place, and it turned into a string, a silver rill winding between. And you followed it as the quilt divided, hopping from pillow to pillow, shouting and slipping and crying out. It led right into the black trees.

All of a sudden, the ragged spikes were around them.

"Robbie?" Fristeen eyed him anxiously.

"I think it's okay," he whispered. It seemed important not to speak loudly.

The trees were silent, without leaves that clapped in the wind or hummed in the breeze. Some grew straight up, but most of them leaned. The only sound was the ringing of the rills, silver and distant. Whatever enchantment they might have felt among the aspen and birch, a far deeper spell lay over these. Robbie felt it powerfully. It wasn't a place for whimsy. You wouldn't find shade or safety. You felt only unease. Your eyes searched—and you searched your mind—for something familiar. But everything here seemed foreign: unheard-of, unthought-of, unknown.

"I'll mark the way," he said.

A taller tree stood in the clear a few paces forward. He sloshed over to it. The spruce was leaning badly—weak, dizzy. Or drawn by something invisible—who could say? Its arms were short and spiky, its trunk was scabbed with ashen flakes. Robbie pulled a sock from his pocket and tied it to a branch.

Cuck. Cuck.

A bird called in the stillness. Robbie turned. Through the black spikes, he caught the flash of calm water. He held his finger to his lips and motioned to Fristeen, and the two of them crept through the leaning trees.

Cuck. Cuck.

The twigs of the spruce were tangled and matted, like your hair when it's dirty and needs to be washed. Some of their arms were twisted, some broken and hanging. Were they like the trees with leaves? If you put your hand to their trunks, would you hear their thoughts? Maybe you wouldn't want to get that close. Maybe they were thoughts you didn't want to hear. They stood apart from each other, and their branches didn't touch. Maybe they didn't share their thoughts, even with other trees.

They came upon a channel with water flashing within. It led straight toward the shore of a glowing lake. They followed it. Grass bunched up and the black trees stood back. A curtain of reeds. Robbie stepped up to it, pushed his fingers through and drew the reeds apart. And there was the Pool.

It was a bowl, and the water in it was red. The hills rolled down to it, and then rolled back up on its far shore. The clouds had spun a thick basket above it, and a single wand of sun jabbed through.

"It's a needle," Fristeen said, pointing to where the ray touched the surface.

Robbie nodded. The Pool was a lens of blood. And in that lens was a world of secrets: turbid mud and coiling breeze, hidden hummocks where silver eels nested, while on the surface water bugs skittered and swept, scribing an alien prophecy in ciphers. On one side, the Pool's surface was rimmed by glowing platinum; on the other, by black trees growing upside down.

At their feet, oily rainbows scalloped the mud. Fristeen knelt and so did Robbie, and they put their fingers in and made the rainbows loop and swirl.

Cuck. Cuck.

They jumped. The bird was ten feet away: black with a yellow eye, perched on an overhanging branch, staring at Fristeen. As they watched, its attention shifted to the reeds. Something was rattling there.

A pair of dragonflies hovered among the shoots, wings whirring. Their long bodies glittered lemon and turquoise, beaded as if they had risen a moment before from the depths of the Pool.

"Look at their eyes," Robbie whispered.

They were giant globes, swollen to bursting, cyan and gold in fluid swirls. But opaque, unfathomable.

The dragonflies fixed suddenly on other business. They darted like thoughts across the scarlet water and into the black trees.

Fristeen sighed.

Robbie yawned and glanced around. The spot behind the reeds was flat and dry.

She read his mind and scooted back. Then she smiled and stretched out.

Robbie lay down beside her and they fell asleep.

Something called Robbie back from a harrowing dream. He awoke, dizzy and muddled, eyes searching for some reassuring sight. Above him was a deep gray sky, and in its center there was a cavern of light, so dim and constricted by clouds that it might have been the moon. He shuddered and rolled over, rising to his knees.

"Fristeen?"

His vision was blurred, but he could see her beside him. He shuddered again, thrown back for a moment into his dream. It *was* a dream, wasn't it? Needles from the heavens pricked him endlessly, and a horde of dragonflies held him down while his blood fed the Pool.

"Fristeen," Robbie whispered. He was in the present now. The cavern of light was what remained of the sun, the encircling clouds staging a gloomy dusk. He recognized the spot of grass they had bedded down on. Fristeen's eyes were opening.

He heard a voice. Nearby or at a distance, he couldn't tell. A sigh sounded from across the Pool.

Fristeen was staring at him. She lifted her head.

Another exhale, sharp and urgent. Then muttering, labored, unintelligible.

Robbie crawled forward, parting the reeds. Fristeen's face poked through beside his.

The far shore of the Pool was marbled with shadow.

Another sharp breath. Then something moved in the brush. Shapes, dark shapes. One had broad shoulders. It might have been a man, standing. In the dim light, his body glinted like the Pool. His chest was silhouetted above the brush. He had the tallest head Robbie had ever seen. A second shape was crawling at his feet—an animal on all fours. It had long hair, like a woman kneeling. The silhouettes were silent, and then the woman rocked and the tall-headed man groaned. As they pulled apart, Robbie saw what she was doing.

A muffled gasp sounded beside him. Fristeen could see it too.

Robbie felt her hand on his arm. Fristeen was trembling.

The man began to groan again.

Robbie's face was burning. His stomach felt sick. "She's eating it," he said. Why didn't the man fight back?

"No. It's still there."

The Pool turned slowly, brimming with blood. Robbie rubbed his eyes and took a breath. Fristeen was right.

"They're gigantic." Fristeen's voice was full of portent.

Robbie didn't understand. And then he realized: the tall-headed man was growing. And so was the woman. Their dark silhouettes rose out of the black trees, into the cold slate of the sky.

With an insistent huff, the man stooped and laid hold of the woman. He rose, growing hugely, his chest expanding, head thrusting like a giant stovepipe. He seemed full of rage. He was lifting her up. The woman spread her arms, but they weren't arms—they were thick and broad, and they batted the air like wings. What did the man intend—to crush her in midair? Hurl her to the ground? The spectral light fell on the gap between them. Robbie felt Fristeen clutch him. She was shuddering, and he was too. They both could see what the man was going to do.

A jagged moan rose from the impaled woman. Not a human sound. It was a beast crying out, the agony of some wounded creature.

Robbie swung to face Fristeen. "He's killing her. We have to do something."

She nodded with an urgent expression.

A second cry reached them, more desperate than the first. Fristeen put her fingers in her ears. They shouldn't be watching this.

Robbie followed suit, stopping his ears, and they turned together, hurrying back through the grass. As they burst through the shrubs, he saw wild thoughts racing in Fristeen's eyes.

There—the silver ribbon. They followed it through the black trees as quickly as they could. When they reached the viburnums, they paused and looked back.

The giant silhouettes had billowed, edges furred and backlit like roiling clouds. And they continued to inflate, bulbing and rising and changing their shapes. Creatures from another world—spectral and behemoth—met in this hidden place to perform some rite. Something strange and unsuspected, unmeant for human eyes. Why this Pool? Had they found their way over land? Did they live in the black trees? No, they came from the skies, and into the skies they were rising—black cumuli bent around the cavernous sun. The giant man grew monstrous, head mushroomed on top, body bristling with

83

horns, while the woman was torn into ashen plumes, feathers set loose and scattered by the wind. Her moan reached them again—crazed, but this time strangely jubilant, as if some triumph had been won. The sound drifted as they listened, trailing down from the heavens and settling in the black trees.

Fristeen turned and cocked her head with a puzzled look.

Something terrible has happened, Robbie thought. And then he saw in that cavern of light that hung between the perpetrator and the victim, a mind that knew what the giants were doing, and why. Robbie recognized its glimmer—the hints of life within. And from the depths of dream, an indelible voice reached him: "Look into my eye."

They faced the viburnum slope and started up it. By the time they reached the top, they were breathing hard. They didn't stop again till they reached the Two-Tree. They circled it once, then turned to look back.

The Pool was clearly visible, but the giants had vanished. The sky was cloudless, leaden gray around the bowl of sun.

They regarded each other, wondering.

"Maybe it just happened in our minds," Fristeen said.

But they knew it was real.

"What was wrong with his head?" Robbie gave her a disbelieving look.

"I feel sorry for her," Fristeen said.

"He killed her."

Fristeen nodded. "That's what she wanted."

"What do you mean?"

"Didn't you hear? The last time she screamed?"

Robbie could hardly forget. But—

Fristeen shook her head. "That's what she wanted. I'm pretty sure."

Full of foreboding, Robbie's gaze returned to the black trees.

"The strangest place," Fristeen muttered.

Robbie nodded. "Too Far."

"Remember what He Knows said," Fristeen reminded him.

The oracle had warned them not to stay late, and it would be evening soon. There was no time to waste.

They descended to Used-to-Be, traversed the Great Place, crossed Trickle and passed beneath the Jigglies. It was there that they felt the first icy drafts. They shivered and traded dark looks, and the looks grew still darker when they reached the Needle Patch. A thin mist was drifting over the Perfect Place. They squirmed through the tunnel, and when they emerged on the far side, they let the scratches go untended and hurried across the meadow. But the mist was thick around the Dot Trees, and Robbie couldn't find the sock.

The chill cut through them. Fristeen's hands began to shake. They were feeling through the branches, looking for the marker. Through an aperture between two alder clumps, Shivers' milky eye appeared, glazed and bulging.

"Where are the birds?" Shivers whispered. He wheezed over them, giant brow curdling, cheeks sagging behind. "And the bugs? There's not a click or a buzz—" He spoke as if to himself. "Is it Shivers they fear?"

85

Robbie held his breath. Fristeen stood motionless beside him. Shivers seemed not to see them. Then the dripping nose shifted, the bulging eyes fixed on them, bloated lips leering.

"Is it *Shivers*?" he hissed. And then he was tittering.

Robbie felt the cold spittle prickling his face.

"Your marker is lost," Shivers observed. "What now?"

Robbie didn't reply.

"You could close your eyes and climb into the fog." Shivers' stringy chin coiled around a Dot Tree.

Robbie remained mute.

"Or you could wait for—conditions to improve?" Shivers sniggered. His chin snaked through the leaves, circling Fristeen.

Robbie's chest spasmed with chills. Fristeen's lips were turning blue.

"Poor children." A greasy tongue wagged out of the reeking maw.

"Poor you," Fristeen barked at him.

Shivers' sigh was like a freezer door opening. "I have no tears, so . . . rain must do."

Gray billows were sliding down the slopes toward them. You could hear the drops rattling the leaves. The billows rolled over them, and the rain came pelting down.

"There," Robbie cried. Through the battered alders was a flapping sock.

They scrambled amid the downpour, clinging to the Dot Tree branches, sliding on the wet slope, instantly drenched. A stiff wind blasted over them, numbing them both, but the wind cleared the mist, and again Robbie cried out.

"The ridge—" He clambered up on hands and knees, and Fristeen did the same. They got their feet beneath them and burrowed through the branches, threading up the incline toward Where You Can See. The crest was swimming in fog.

"Robbie, Robbie—"

He yelped, and their desperation turned into breakneck abandon. Wailing and shrieking, they dashed to the high point and along it at full speed, weaving through the drifting muzz. They seemed sure to go plunging down one side or the other—then the mist would shift and they'd spy the way. There—the gate. The gate!

They passed between the stumps, spluttering with relief, clutching each other, hugging and stumbling, rolling down the incline, cheek to cheek. Crying? Laughing? Oh, plenty of each.

As they came to rest, a fierce wind struck the slope. A thick sheaf of litter rumpled before them, built to a wave, then reared straight up. Shivers' sodden features emerged from the pasted leaves.

Fristeen screamed. Robbie staggered back. Shivers hung there, ravening them, eye orbits sucking, his prehensile chin snapping at the ground like a whip.

"A great romance in the offing," Shivers croaked. "'*Can I see yours?*'" His humor was gone.

"You're in our way," Robbie bellowed.

"More than you know," Shivers said venomously. "I'm your goose bumps, and—" to Fristeen "—your peachfuzz pricking up." Then to both: "I'm the shivers between you. Every sigh, every giggle passes through *me*."

"You nasty old man—" Fristeen shook with rage.

"Your sage chaperone," Shivers corrected her.

Robbie grabbed Fristeen's hand and struggled forward. They had to cross the stream. Shivers' maw opened and a torrent of mulch whirled out. Through the flying leaves, Robbie caught sight of the log. As they scrambled toward it, Shivers' great visage flew apart. Robbie reached the log, straddled it and started across. Fristeen was right behind him.

The wind let them get halfway, and then it came blasting between the banks and the log started bucking. They jockeyed and clung, but the thrashing mounted. Robbie was thrown off and Fristeen let go, and they fell together into the murky stream. The current wasn't strong. Fristeen lifted herself and gave Robbie a hand, and they clambered up the steep bank.

As they reached the top, the rain ceased abruptly and a fog curled round them. Shivers was in it, squeezing their soaked bodies with icy claws, chilling them to the bone. Robbie heard Fristeen's teeth chattering.

"Cold, little saplings?" Shivers hissed.

"Make him stop," Fristeen begged.

"You're like all the other babes in these woods." Shivers grew mordant. "For a summer, your leaves flutter with another's. You imagine you're kin to the stars. But the same sap that inflames you, freezes and splits you. And the older you grow, the deader at heart."

The mist was impenetrable. Robbie's hands were numb. He knew he was stumbling forward—he could see his thighs moving. But his legs had lost their feeling. They seemed no longer to belong to him. *Is this what it's like?* he wondered. *When you're about to die?* One hand stretched back to someone who cares for you, the other reaching for a place you can't see. In your ears, the rustle of limbs against leaves, audible shadows in the land of the blind.

"Call it love if you like," Shivers said softly, "but it's just decomposing. You sprouted alone, and you'll wither alone. The only peace in this world is inside me."

"He Knows?" Robbie shouted.

"Close, close, close . . ."

"Are we near the edge?"

"Wet, wet, wet, wet . . ."

Before Robbie could figure out what He Knows meant, his heel slid on the soaked mulch. He landed at the bottom of a pit on his hip, groaning with pain.

"Robbie!"

Shivers was coiled in the pit with him. Robbie could feel his slimy head probing and stretching, crawling over him like a bloated worm. The stench made him gag. He lurched upright, struggling to stand, clawing his way up the side of the pit. When Fristeen saw him, she grabbed his arm.

"There—" She pointed, leading the way through the brush, putting the stream bed behind them. His hip hurt badly, but he did his best to keep up.

89

When they reached the Fallen Down Trees, they spotted the marker through the mist and scrambled beneath, and when they rose on the far side, it was barely drizzling and the Bendies were in the clear.

"The cloudburst is over. But let's not say farewell." Shivers spoke to their backs. "We're tight now. I've got my gums in you, and I'm starting to chew."

6

By the time they reached the Clearing, the dinner hour was past. Mom would be angry, Robbie knew, and Dad would have to calm her down. He and Fristeen said their goodbyes quickly. So much had happened. The giants across the Pool were still looming before him. And when he put his hand on the doorknob, it was shaking as if Shivers had hold of it. He wasn't certain what he would tell his parents, but he couldn't wait to see them.

When he walked through the door, neither was in the living room. Except for the white candles, the dining table was clear. Robbie glanced through the kitchen entry and saw Mom standing by the sink. She wasn't doing anything, just gazing through the window with a stick of celery in her hand.

"Mom?"

She jumped, then sighed and turned to face him. "Daniel Boone's back," she said, as if from a distance.

"Is Dad here?"

"Not yet."

Robbie saw the covered pots on the stove. "What's for dinner?"

"Linguine casalinga," Mom said. She smiled, coming back to herself. "The way Grandma makes it. Hey—you're drenched." She knelt, regarding him at close range.

Could she see the agitation in his eyes?

Robbie threw himself into her arms and hugged her tightly. So often it seemed that Mom didn't understand. But there were things Mom understood best. Sometimes you just wanted a squishy breast to cry on. Sometimes you didn't want to be brave.

"Oh Robbie—" Mom kissed him and cradled him.

"Will you help me change?"

Mom laughed and nodded, and they started down the hall.

"It gets cold in the forest," he told her. He shivered reflexively. "Know what me and Fristeen found? A place where the trees are black and the water is red."

Mom stepped into his room, sat on his bed and drew him close. "Robbie—" She peered into his eyes, searching. "You still love me. Don't you?"

Mom seemed about to cry.

"Of course, Mom."

"I know you think I'm screwing up. I think so too, sometimes. I'm sorry I'm always forcing rules on you."

Robbie didn't know what to say.

"We thought we wanted the same thing," Mom said.

He patted Mom's hand. She seemed so small.

"It was wonderful. Our little home in California—the rolling hills and the oaks— The weather was warm, and the people—" The words caught in her throat. "It wasn't remote enough for your dad." She paused. "We had our *vision*—"

"The cabin-in-the-wild," Robbie said. "Dad still thinks—"

"I know what Dad thinks," Mom said. She looked beyond him. "I wish you had a wider circle of friends. It's hard to meet other moms. The people here are . . . so different. I guess Alaska is a little more than I can take."

"Mom?"

She met his stare.

"Should I put some dry clothes on?"

"Yes," she smiled, "let's get those things off."

When they finished, they returned to the kitchen and Mom put food on three plates. They carried them to the table and sat down.

They didn't eat right away. They waited. Robbie twisted his fork in the noodles and listened for the sound of Dad's car. Finally, they both started to eat. They didn't say anything and they ate slowly. From time to time, Robbie glanced at Dad's food. You could see steam rising up, and then the steam stopped.

Dad had been late before, but Mom acted like this was different. She was sad when they began to eat, and she got sadder and sadder. She stared at her noodles as if they were all their arguments piled in front of her, tangled together.

When they were done, they bussed the dishes and put Dad's food in the fridge.

Then Mom put him to bed.

Robbie lay there for awhile, listening. He thought he might hear the sound of Dad's car in the drive. But he was wrong. The only sound was Dad's voice echoing in his bedroom. "Goodbye," it said. "Goodbye, goodbye . . ."

Something raised him from his fitful sleep. Robbie opened his eyes and found himself drifting. Not on the ground, but high above it—on his back, facing up. It wasn't day or night. It was a strange mingling of both, like what they'd seen at the Pool. There was a spot of sun, and it was blinding. But it burned at the back of a dismal cave, and the sky all around it was leaden and gloomy. Around the cave's rim, dark cumuli were bent—the ghosts of giants risen—once monstrous, now spent.

"Dream, Robbie. Dream," a deep voice said.

Robbie peered into the cave, and saw thoughts stirring within.

"I'm here," the Dream Man said. "Looking down from heaven. At the back of your mind."

The cave was an eye, a cauldron glowing and alive—a brazier of embers, lemon and blue, coals beat to powder, circling,

circling. And the cauldron was tipping, daring to pour, and Robbie was soaring, lifted straight toward it.

"Where am I?" he wondered.

"Look down," the Dream Man replied.

In the spectral light, Robbie saw the black trees.

"The place you disappear to—when you dream."

"I've never—"

"Oh you have, you have," the Dream Man assured him. "You just don't recall."

The deep voice was smiling. It wanted to soothe him, but Robbie was scared. A rushing sound reached him, some fury of motion from the churning eye. Was it powder? Liquid? A hurricane of stars? Or rivers of minnows in a giant jar?

"Are you real?" Robbie asked.

"Are thoughts real?" the Dream Man mused. "Would I be any less real if I lived only in your mind?"

Robbie kept rising and the rushing grew louder. The giant eye was opening wider and wider, the strange element within seething and sparking as it turned before him, seeing him, knowing him as no mere human might.

"Are you dreaming? Right now?" the Dream Man asked him.

"I guess I am."

"Is your body along?"

"No. It's at home. In bed."

"It's a mercy the gold can be drawn from the rock. That body on the bed is a frail little thing. The world it clings to is better off shed. Look, Robbie," the Dream Man said softly. There was care in his voice, care and love. "Look into my eye. What matters more—your brain, your head, or the ideas inside?"

The first spinning streams left the cauldron flying, and a pinwheel of turquoise and gold lit up the cloudy gray.

"A new universe," the Dream Man said. "Remember?"

The eye seemed to explode, a great whirling galaxy of stretching stars— No, dragonflies! An uncontainable horde, spinning and glittering, batting feverish wings—a furious mind with a billion ideas, each taking its own path to a new reach of the sky.

"That's what you want, isn't it?" The Dream Man boomed. "To set your spirit loose? To wander perfectly free?"

The Dream Man knew. Robbie wanted that more than anything in the world.

"To go wherever thought leads?" This last, the Dream Man spoke with great fondness, like a blessing.

Robbie felt such joy, he thought his heart would burst. The first dragonflies struck him, and were dashed into jewels that burned and smoked.

"Do I have it?" asked the Dream Man.

"Have what?" Robbie cried.

"The idea," the Dream Man said.

The great cauldron loomed closer, and the living whirlpool churned. The rushing of wings deafened Robbie's senses—

"What idea?" Robbie murmured.

The Dream Man laughed. "The idea of you."

Robbie sat up in bed. It was morning, and sun was filtering through his curtains.

Something was wrong.

His arm was gone. He glanced down. He could see it on the blanket beside him, but he couldn't feel it, and when he told it to move, nothing happened. Had Shivers frozen it in the night? *It's probably asleep.* They did that sometimes—arms and legs. Then another thought struck him.

It's in Too Far. That frightened Robbie badly.

He leaped out of bed and grabbed his toothbrush with his good arm. The other was tingling. Was it trying to get back? Did it even care?

That thought frightened Robbie the most. His dream was still with him—as real as life. Above the black trees, the cauldron was brewing. The Dream Man's voice boomed over the humming wings. Robbie's thoughts were as frenzied as the dragonfly swarms, and he felt a great welling as he gazed into the whirling eye. "That's what you want, isn't it?" the Dream Man had said.

To go to Too Far, and never come back— That's what he meant.

Robbie's arm had returned. He raised it in the mirror, used a finger to pick his nose. Then he spit out the toothpaste, washed his face, and examined the bruise on his hip.

When he stepped into the hall, Mom was standing by the table. She smiled and poured out some cereal for him.

"Sleep well?" she asked.

"Yep," he replied. Mom's hair was lopsided, and her face looked gray. "What about you?"

"Hardly at all," she said quietly.

"Where's Dad?"

Mom's shadowed eyes shifted.

Was she going to speak? No, she was too upset.

Dad hadn't come home.

They ate breakfast in silence.

It was hard to look at Mom. Robbie shifted to the side and shut one eye, and one of the candles blocked her out.

"It's your vacation," he said finally.

Mom nodded. "I'm off till next week."

"What are you going to do?"

"Mend some of the clothing. Clean the oven—"

"That's no fun."

Mom heard the disdain in his voice, and put her toast down. "Do you know what it means—to 'take someone for granted'?"

Robbie laughed, rising. "That's what Dad and I do."

Mom saw the pity in his eyes and the plea for forgiveness. "Oh honey—"

They stood together and hugged. Then Robbie helped clear the dishes.

They had almost finished when there was a knock at the back door. Robbie's heart leaped.

"I'll get it." He sprang through the living room, grabbed the knob and opened the door wide. And there they were—big and beautiful—Fristeen's eyes, eager to see him. But the rest of her was shy. She peered around Robbie, risking a smile, afraid to step forward. Should he invite her in? Then he thought about Mom—how miserable she was—and changed his mind.

"I'm going out," Robbie called over his shoulder.

Mom saw the visitor. For a long moment, she stared at her without speaking. "Alright," she said. "Both of you—take care."

Robbie motioned to Fristeen and closed the door behind him. As they crossed the deck, Fristeen gave him a worried look. She knew something was wrong.

"My mom's really sad," he explained. "I am too." He took a breath. "Last night, Dad didn't come home."

Fristeen nodded. She knew what that was like. "When Dada left, I thought, *I'll never be happy again.* I couldn't stop crying."

She cleared the hair from his eyes. Robbie wondered if she was going to tell him everything would be fine. But Fristeen knew better.

"I just cried and cried," she said. "And Grace cried too—even though she didn't love Dada anymore. '*Who cares*—' That's what Grace said. But she really did care. '*Who cares*—'" Fristeen shook her head.

"*Who cares,*" Robbie imitated her. It didn't help. "How old were you?"

"Five," she said.

They crossed the Clearing and started up the Hill.

Fristeen reached for his hand.

99

A stray breeze circled them.

"Is your dada going to come back?" Fristeen asked.

Robbie watched his shoes crunch the litter. "I hope so." He shrugged.

"Mine isn't," Fristeen said.

When they arrived on top, she stopped and faced him.

"Robbie—" Her eyes flared.

He could see she'd been holding something inside.

"You won't believe—" Her arms scissored excitedly.

"What?"

"Last night—I didn't sleep at all. I figured it out—"

He gave her a puzzled look.

"I know who that giant is—the lady."

Robbie was amazed. "You do?"

Fristeen nodded and licked her lips, eager to explain. "I've seen her before—lots of times. I didn't recognize her at first. She never showed me her wings. It was her cry—that last sound she made—"

Robbie frowned, confused.

"That's how I knew. It was her! Really. I'm sure." She grabbed his arm and shook it, laughing. "That first day I saw you? It was Dawn who told me to wander that way—"

"Dawn?"

Fristeen smiled. "That's her name." There was so much to share. "When I talk to you at night? Dawn's there with us. She thinks you're great. She's been watching you for a long time. When you were in your mom's tummy, she made sure you came out. She loves you as much as I do—" Fristeen's eyes brimmed. She leaned toward him, then stopped herself, blushed, and reached a finger up to touch his cheek.

"Dawn's your secret friend," Robbie said.

"Yes." Fristeen hopped on her toes. "But don't you see? She's not secret anymore. I thought Dawn was just for me, in private. But you saw her too! She's here—" Fristeen gazed around them with astonishment. "In real life."

"You're certain it was her?"

"Yes— She told me."

"Told you?"

"She came to me, Robbie. Early this morning. When it was just starting to be light."

"You were dreaming."

"It's sort of like dreaming," she furrowed her brow. "Or like when you're awake, using your extra-seeing powers. She comes at night or early in the morning, when I'm in bed—" She bit her lip and looked up at him. "Oh Robbie—" Fristeen beamed. "She's the most beautiful woman in the world. If you were married to Dawn, you'd never want to leave her. She's like the sun—love pours out of her. It just pours and pours."

"Wow," Robbie said. What Fristeen had told him—at first, it didn't make sense. But now, it made more sense than he could have imagined.

"What is it?" She saw the stunned look in his face.

"I had a dream too," he said.

"Really?"

He nodded. "I saw the man."

Fristeen's jaw dropped. "With the head that's too tall?"

"Yep. He came and got me last night when I was sleeping. The Dream Man."

"The Dream Man?" Fristeen whispered.

"He's the god of Too Far."

Fristeen was dumbstruck. Then the truth blossomed in her eyes. "She's in love with him."

They stood there imagining it. A sigh passed through the aspens high above.

"Are you sure?" Robbie frowned.

"Sure of what?"

"It seemed like he was hurting her. Really bad."

Fristeen shook her head. "It was just like I said. Dawn told me. She wanted him to. But she wouldn't say why. Embarrassed, I bet." Fristeen giggled. "She's mad about the Dream Man and his spooky brain."

It was a perfect day and the woods were inviting, but when they hunched beneath the Bendies, they felt like bending all the way. It had been a busy night and they were both exhausted, especially Fristeen. So when they reached the Fallen Down Trees, they crawled inside and took a nap. Robbie had another dream—a funny one, for a change.

He dreamt he was wandering in the forest with Fristeen. They came upon a weathered log. It was like Used-to-Be, except that it had broken off five feet above the ground, and was still clinging to its stump. As they passed, the log shifted and Mom's face rose from its ragged shoulder.

"Well, hello," Mom said with a cheery smile. "Where have *you* been?"

"That's not your business," Fristeen replied.

Mom shrugged her shoulder. "Just curious." She looked from Fristeen to Robbie. She seemed genuinely interested.

Robbie gave Fristeen a wink. "Ask away."

Mom saw the displeasure in Fristeen's face. "I don't get around much," she explained with an unassuming expression.

"That's a shame," Fristeen said drily.

"Before the storm, I had a fine view." Mom glanced up the bole of a nearby birch. "I can't see much now, with my top in the dirt. I miss having leaves." Her sigh turned into a laugh. "Oh, I'm the happy sort. There's always something going on, right here." Her eyes flashed. "This break in my side? Rain leaked through it. Conks grew on my bark. Then ants arrived. They built a fine nest, which brought woodpeckers. See these holes? *That* was exciting." Mom laughed. "Well, you see what I mean." She gazed around her. "All these unbroken trees— they've got more to look at. And with legs, you go anywhere you please." She eyed Fristeen with admiration. "That's my dream."

Fristeen nodded at Robbie. How could they be mean to her? "What can we tell you?" Fristeen said.

"What about yesterday?" Mom wondered.

"You had to be there," Robbie laughed.

Mom groaned.

"We climbed a slope," Robbie told her. "And at the top there was a tree with two trunks. Then we found a way down the other side—"

"And?"

"And we reached this forest with a lot of black trees."

"Black?" Mom frowned. "Do they come in black?"

"Yep. Gods live there."

"Big as clouds—" Fristeen chimed in.

"They do whatever they think of," Robbie told Mom.

"Such as—" Mom's eyes were wide.

"They go naked," Robbie said, "and they grunt—"

"—and scream—" Fristeen said.

"And some die—"

"But they want to—" Fristeen started laughing.

"And some have tall heads." Now Robbie was laughing. "Their brains never stop growing—"

"How could—" Mom caught her breath. "Why would they—" Her gaze shifted from side to side, as if something ominous was advancing on her. "I have so many questions— It's a bit confusing." Her head was sliding back behind her shoulder. "I'm going to have to think about this."

They continued along.

"Poor thing," Fristeen said.

"'*They built a fine nest*,'" Robbie recalled Mom's words. "She's just sawdust inside."

A stillness descended on the forest.

"She's got a good attitude," Fristeen said.

When they awoke, it was late in the day. Clouds were gathering, and He Knows had his doubts, so they returned to the Bendies and explored on their bellies. There were a hundred exotic things to see: green shield bugs and striped flies, little plants with pairs of pink bells, and flowers that were tiny white stars. You could lick your fingernails and the stars would stick. Then they found a plant that had ears like a rabbit, so they whispered Too Far secrets in them, and plugged them with grass.

It was a great afternoon.

And it was a great night, too. When Robbie got home, Dad was there.

It was like Dad had never been gone. No, it was better than that. It was like before Mom and Dad started arguing.

Dad ran out onto the deck and picked him up and spun him around by his arms.

"Dad's back—" Mom was gleeful. "Dad's back."

Then Mom kissed Dad—Robbie saw her gratitude and relief. Dad laughed and said, "I missed you both so much." He kissed Robbie and Mom, and then Mom kissed Robbie, and they had a group hug.

"Look at *us*," Mom said, taking in the three of them, the house, and the Hill with its trees. "We really have something here." She gave Dad a wistful look.

Dad smiled a real smile. "We haven't done too bad."

"And for dinner," Mom said, rolling her eyes, "we've got everybody's favorite—macaroni and cheese."

"Great," Robbie shouted, and they went inside.

They all helped carry the food to the table, and when they sat down, Robbie let Mom serve him, like she did when he was younger. Dad said the prayer his own mom had taught him, and Robbie remembered it and backed him up. They hadn't done that together for a really long time. They ate and they talked, and—best of all—there wasn't a moment that Dad sank from sight. You could see everything in his face—he was all outside.

"Where were you today?" Dad asked.

"Same old place," Robbie said. "How about you?"

"Mm?"

"Last night," Robbie said.

"Oh, same old place," Dad laughed. "At the department. You have to do that if you want to be a doc. Sometimes you work all night long. Hey, I've got an idea. Tomorrow—let's go to Creamer's Field."

"That would be wonderful," Mom said. "Wouldn't it, Robbie?"

"Sure."

"The geese," Mom said. "Remember?"

"Yep. They're great," Robbie nodded. The geese were for toddlers, but why spoil the fun?

For a moment, his parents' voices faded. Robbie imagined picking up his old life where it had left off. There wasn't any world beyond the Clearing, and his only playmates were kids like Jim. He brushed his teeth, and it wasn't so bad, because Dad was with him, talking as they brushed, and they were talking about brains and nerves, and things they both liked so much. Mom was cheerful, and she wasn't so tired that she wanted to sleep all the time. And at night, they'd talk about the cabin-in-the-wild Dad would build some day. It was a simple life, like the one Mom-the-log led in his dream. Robbie basked in the memory of it, but he knew it was all pretend. Things weren't going to be like that again.

He hoped Mom and Dad would be happy, of course. But he wasn't the same Robbie, and it wasn't just that he was older. He'd changed. He was self-reliant, and he'd learned how to be brave. He'd been tested by Shivers, and crossed into Too Far. He was in love with Fristeen, and he lived now to explore.

The Robbie that Mom and Dad knew— He was gone.

"I'll get dessert," Mom said, rising.

"Dad and I agree—" Robbie glanced at Dad. "We're lucky to have a mom like you."

"Robbie—" Mom blushed.

When she turned, Robbie gave Dad a meaning look.

As Mom's footsteps faded, Dad regarded him uncertainly.

"Mom got pretty upset," Robbie said. "I had to calm her down."

Dad seemed at a loss for words. "Thanks," he said at last.

7

For Robbie, the days that followed were serene.

Dad's return ushered in a new era of harmony, and the little house was, once again, a welcoming place.

Mom read one of the books Jim's mom had given her. She sat on the sofa and disappeared into her thoughts, and that made her happy. Afterward, when she shared her thoughts with Dad, he smiled. Robbie wondered if he was just being nice, but then he looked at her that special way and kissed her temple. Dad only did that when he loved what you were thinking.

One night after dinner, Mom was putting the wash away.

"Robbie?" She was calling from his room, and she sounded flustered.

"What?"

Mom stood by his dresser. "Your socks are gone."

"I used them," he confessed, "to mark the way."

The most amazing thing happened—Mom didn't get angry.

"You'll need some new ones. For markers, I've got clothes we can shred. Loud colors? Or is white better?"

Robbie's leash remained long and loose, and he had no cause to tug on it. He was with Fristeen nearly every day. They talked about Dawn and the Dream Man a lot.

Robbie told Fristeen all he knew about the Dream Man. How commanding he was, but gentle too. He lifted you like a tuft of willow down, and bore you away without hurting you in the least. Robbie figured out what happened to the Dream Man's head. He didn't have a skull, like people do. It was more like a jar. And it didn't have a top, it was open to the air. So his dreams could go anywhere, any time—they weren't trapped inside his mind.

"He's so *serious,*" Fristeen said. "Dawn likes him that way."

They were climbing through the scrub one day, headed for the Great Place. A breeze was at their backs, and Fristeen was humming like she so often did.

"I like it when you hum," Robbie told her.

"I can hear Dawn's song," Fristeen said, "in the wind and the leaves. When Dawn is singing, I hum along." There was reverence in her voice. This was one of Dawn's deepest secrets.

"Whenever you're happiest, Dawn remembers. She hears the little sounds you make, and puts them in a song. Not what you say. Just, those *little* sounds." Fristeen's voice softened. "I hear *us* when Dawn sings. You and me, Robbie. Because of her, everything good that happens never goes away."

They crossed the Great Place in silence, and climbed the slope above Used-to-Be. The Two-Tree rose before them. They approached it and peered down.

The green viburnums descended. The black trees spread out. And there was the Pool, blood-red in the sun.

"Dawn married him," Fristeen said. "That's what we saw."

Robbie thought about that.

"They're together now," she mused, scanning the hills.

"Or off on a dream," Robbie said.

"I can hear her singing," Fristeen reminded him.

"Want to go down?"

A stray breeze struck them and sent shivers up their backs.

"It's their honeymoon," Fristeen said, considering. "They want time to themselves."

So they turned away. During the two weeks that followed, they returned to the Two-Tree, but they didn't enter the black trees. It wasn't that they were afraid— They didn't want to bother Dawn and her Dream Man. And it was so blissful in the realm of green leaves.

It was hot in late June, and still hotter in July. They were masters of their kingdom now, all the places they knew so well. They sighed and sank into them, wearing them like soft pajamas, content to idle and laze. They would stretch out beneath the Jigglies with honey on their fingers, and the lemon butterflies would come to perch and dance. Or they'd sit and rock together atop Where You Can See, and watch the wind sweep in waves through the mirror trees. The leaves were shards that each gust would shake, and the crowns heaved like swells on a shattered lake.

The forest continued to change. The Dot branches were so bushy, you could barely climb through them. Spikes rose from the fireweed around Used-to-Be, and magenta blooms burst out. The canopy got so thick, the forest was like one big tree. When you looked up at the trunks, you couldn't tell which boughs bore the leaves.

One day, Robbie decided it was time to climb a tree to its top. They stood in the Great Place together, gazing up, and imagined how he might. But there was nothing to hold onto—even the lowest Great branches were impossibly high. They settled for the Bendies and found one with knobs, and he shinnied halfway up it, hanging on for his life. A breeze caught him and he cried out, Fristeen screaming below, and the bough swung him wildly, heart racing, eyes dazzled— It was a victory and they celebrated, whirling till they swooned. And then they shouted out the details, and He Knows spread the news.

At night, Robbie opened his window and fell asleep to the sounds—ticks and chirrups, shrills and caws. Was the Dream Man with him? In the late hours, a distant echo eddied in Robbie's ear. A memory, most likely. Dawn didn't visit Fristeen, but for her also, there was a mysterious reminder outside. After hours white and blinding, the sun dipped for a brief time and painted pictures of Dawn with orange juice and jam. Like postcards from far away. When either of them got one, they would share it. They spoke of their gods fondly, as if they were relatives in the States.

Then the rain came. And with it, came trouble. Not so much for Robbie. At home, the merriment had faded, but his parents seemed at peace. Things were busy at the lab, and Mom was scribbling in her journal like she used to. But Fristeen was upset with Grace, and Robbie had to help her through that. They spent every day together, and they had the house to themselves. Grace was gone a lot—even at bedtime, or in the morning when Fristeen got up. Fristeen didn't know how to cook or do the wash, and it was creepy being in the house all night by yourself.

"Grace just doesn't care," Fristeen would say. Then she'd be sorry she was angry, and feel bad about that. Grace was a great mom, in lots of ways. When she was gone, she didn't forget you. She'd bring back some kind of surprise. And even when you were furious, she didn't get angry herself. She just wanted to make up.

It rained for six days, and on the sixth, Robbie rose early and left first thing. As he crossed the deck, he recalled the week he'd spent fogging the window. What a baby he'd been. You put on your jacket and go where you like. If it rains, you get wet. Simple as that.

Fristeen was waiting. They hugged and kidded, and then huddled in her room with crayons and birch curls they'd found in the Great Place. The bark was like paper, and when you flattened it on the floor, you could write your thoughts down. It even had lines. When they finished, they fished Robbie's bow and arrows out from under her bed. They'd taped an ugly likeness on the laundry room closet, and the prize was a kiss if you hit Shivers' nose.

After that, they sat by the window and played "Follow Your Thoughts." Of the games they'd invented, Robbie liked that one best.

"It's okay indoors. But I'd rather be outside." He eyed the wet woodland through the speckled pane.

"Me too," Fristeen nodded.

"It's safer here. The forest can be dangerous."

She made her eyes wide and grinned.

Robbie laughed. "It's fun to think about things that scare you—before they happen. Or after they've scared you, when you know you're safe. But right when it's happening—"

Fristeen understood. "It's no fun at all."

"Isn't that strange?"

Just then, someone banged on the front door.

They stared at each other. The banging came again.

"Angel?" a man growled.

"Duane," Fristeen said.

"Pretend we're not here."

Fristeen shook her head.

She strode toward the door and Robbie followed. Fristeen twisted the knob, budged the door and peered through the gap.

"Where's Grace?" Duane said.

Beneath the black slash of hair, Robbie saw the suspicious eyes shift, trying to look inside. Duane's shiny coat was streaming. He was soaked. The rain hissed on the hot parts of his motorcycle, parked in a puddle on the drive.

"She's not home," Fristeen told him.

"Open the door."

Fristeen quivered. "You can't come in."

"Shit for breakfast—" Through the gap, Robbie saw Duane's coat swell, then the little animals inside it were yapping and squealing, and the hair on Duane's head was whipping back and forth. "It's raining out here!"

Fristeen was wide-eyed. "You can't come in," she yelled, holding the knob tight.

Duane kicked the door with his knee.

"If you brought something," Fristeen said, "slip it through."

A moment of silence. Duane stepped to one side and neither could see him. They waited, breathless, listening to the rain. Then a brown pill bottle pushed through the gap.

"Save a few for Grace," Duane said.

Fristeen didn't respond.

"We're in love, you know," Duane added drily.

"You'll do anything for nookie," Fristeen said with contempt.

Another silence.

"You're right about that," Duane muttered.

More silence. He cursed and kicked the door again.

Then they heard the gravel crunching.

A moment later, Duane's motorcycle rumbled away through the rain.

Robbie was pale. "What's nookie?"

"I don't know. Something Grace has." Fristeen raised the pill bottle. "'*Duane is special*,'" she mimicked her mother. "The only thing special about him is these."

She hurled the pill bottle down, and red capsules sprayed across the floor.

Robbie saw Fristeen's face twist into a fearsome mask, then she shrieked and lunged, kicking mattresses and blankets aside. When she reached the kitchen door, she beat her fists against it. Then she stopped and wrenched it open. Robbie followed her in, stunned, unsure what to do.

Fristeen swept her arm toward a package of soup crackers on the counter, and they went flying around the room. Then she jumped onto a stool and flung the cupboard doors open. A can of beans and a jar of peanut butter—that was it.

"She's so busy!" Fristeen raged. "She always *thinks* she's in love—" Her fists were clenched, her arms crashed onto the cupboard shelf. "But she never is!" She pounded the shelf again and again.

Then she drew a stuttering breath and her arms went limp.

Robbie thought she might fall. He reached out and grabbed her. She was shaking. As he helped her down off the stool, she turned her face away.

"We'll figure it out," Robbie said. She felt weak and helpless in his arms.

Then she started to cry.

He ran his fingers over the tail of her eye.

"When Grace gets happy," Fristeen whimpered, "she's just happy for herself. She forgets about everyone else."

"Don't worry about food—"

Fristeen gazed at him. "I want to see Dawn."

Robbie glanced through the window. The rain had stopped. "We can if we want."

She clasped his hand. "Let's go right now."

And that's what they did.

A few shreds of mist were drifting through the woods, but by the time they reached the Dot Trees, it had all burned off. With Shivers out of mind and a clear blue sky, Robbie made a beeline for Trickle. Fristeen remained silent, prey to dark thoughts. As they rose on the far side of the Needle Patch, she faced him with a nervous look.

"The Dream Man's the most important thing for her now. But she still loves *us,* and she wants us to be with her. With *them,* I mean. The Dream Man, too."

Then she lapsed into silence until they were on the slope below the Great Place. A breeze was blowing through a stand of small birch, and an orange scarf seemed carried along with it. It floated over the ground and disappeared among the trees.

They stared at each other.

"A fox," Robbie whispered.

Fristeen's eyes sparkled. "Look," she pointed.

117

The branches of the birch were glowing with silver bands.

"Dawn put rings on their fingers." Fristeen smiled. "She always does those kind of things."

Robbie leaned close and squeezed her hand.

When the Two-Tree appeared, it was glorious with leaves. And as they approached the twin trunks, Too Far opened before them. Its mossy hills rolled amber and chartreuse, and silver ribbons connected its blood-red lakes. With all that summer had done to the green woodland, Too Far was exactly the same. Black trees don't change.

"If Dawn knew—" Fristeen spoke beneath her breath. "I don't blame her. She's out of touch, with her wedding and all." She glanced at Robbie, and together their gazes went to the far shore of the Pool.

"Let's go down," Fristeen said.

Robbie led the way.

They descended through the viburnum, reached the moss pillows, and followed the rill. The moss was bloated and gushed beneath their feet. When they reached the first of the spindly spruce, Robbie held his fingers to his lips and they crept toward the reeds. He parted the green curtain and the Pool appeared.

They scanned it quickly, and then with more care. The Dream Man and Dawn were nowhere to be seen.

It was cooler this time. No blackbird. No dragonflies. It was strangely quiet.

"Scared?" Robbie murmured.

Fristeen nodded. She stood staring at the far shore. Then she glanced at Robbie and started around the Pool's rim.

What's the idea? Robbie wondered. He followed behind. With small steps at first, and then more assuredly, they circled the Pool. There were lines on the water, all going one way; and other lines, going the opposite way; together they formed a fluid mesh, and you couldn't stop staring at it—once it had you, it wouldn't let go. A gnarled shape appeared on the surface. As they approached, Robbie imagined some creature huddled there. He waited for the thing to rise and confront them. But the shape didn't move. All remained still.

They came around the far side. Fristeen paused at the water's edge, eyeing the red glass. Bugs etched the surface, as before, using ciphers only the gods of Too Far understood.

"Have a taste," she murmured, kneeling. She skimmed her hand and sipped.

Robbie did the same. It was sweet.

"Touch the bottom," she said. She thrust her arm all the way down.

Robbie followed her lead.

The red climbed to your wrist, to your elbow, and higher. It was cold and tingly.

"Feel it?" Fristeen whispered. "Close your eyes."

It was soft as oatmeal. It crept through your fingers like something alive.

"They were there," Fristeen said.

Robbie looked up.

Her dripping hand pointed to a hump of higher ground.

They stood and stepped toward it.

The flank of the low rise was bare soil. An iridescent slime oozed from it, collecting below. They waded through the muck and climbed the rise. At the top, there was a thick mat of emerald moss. To the side, a stand of sedge had been bent back.

Fristeen studied the ground, then turned and scanned the surrounding hills and the sky. She stepped over to a shrub and pulled a pair of broad leaves from a branch.

"Sometimes you're afraid, when you're alone or it's dark." Fristeen spoke without looking at him. "Or when you're trying to find her. But when Dawn comes, you aren't."

"What—"

"You're going to meet her," Fristeen said softly. "I hope." She smiled and gestured with the leaves in her hand. "I'm going to lay here. You'll be there." She pointed at the bed of moss.

She approached his spot.

Robbie followed. "It's kind of wet."

She nodded. "That's okay. Right here."

What were they doing? Robbie knelt in the moss. Would Dawn really come?

"Stretch out on your back," she said.

Robbie did as she directed. The spongy surface gave beneath him, soaking the back of his shirt and pants.

"I'll put these on your eyes."

The leaves settled, dimming the glare.

"I'm going to call her," Fristeen said. "It's a secret way she taught me. Promise you won't peek."

"I promise."

"Ready?" she whispered.

Robbie nodded, then he heard the moss crush by his ear, and her steps drew away.

A little time passed. He felt the sun on his front. The cool water tickled his back.

"I'm here," Fristeen's voice reached him from a short distance. "I'm going to start."

Then more time passed. Robbie sighed. Whatever Fristeen was doing, it wasn't working.

Through his leaf spectacles, the sun was an amorphous glow. All he could see was a broad field of gold. As he watched, it seemed to quiver. Was it the light, or his lid twitching? There was a sound, too. Plaintive, like a rabbit's whimper, from way up there. As he listened, it descended—a simple strand, pure and transparent, falling from the sky.

Closer it came, closer, closer— It struck Robbie where he lay, dashing into a million jewels! Dawn's voice opened like a powerful bouquet, a basket of sweet fruits, peeled and glittering, filling the air with all those moments she remembered, all the happiness that never goes away.

Dawn was singing. And she was breathing, too. Breathing joy in, and breathing it out again, pulsing the air with fanning wings. Where had she come from? Robbie could see her through the leaf lenses, wings wide, dripping with gold. Her great feathers whistled and hummed and stuttered as she hovered, rubbing against each other, loosing joys and herding them together. A squeaky shoe skipping, chirps like a sparrow's, a kitten's mew. Gasps, warbles, purrs and tremolos— All those voices danced around him. And then—he could hear his own!

Sounds of happiness filled his chest to bursting! He was curled in a ball. He was leaping with his arms and legs rayed like a star! He was a spear, hurtling through space, his nose sharp as a blade— The air was hot froth, and the ground beneath him, too. Dawn's long pinions beat deeply, drawing him up. The world let go and Robbie rose with her, held by nothing but a surge of love. An endless cascade, just like Fristeen said, flowing and flowing. All Dawn wanted was to pour her love out.

They were perfectly together in a moment entirely apart.

Then the flow outpaced him. The jeweled voices broke away. *Please, don't leave—* But gravity was returning. Dawn had let go of him, and the joys were fading. He could hear her great wings sighing through the trees.

Robbie felt himself rocking in a cradle of moss, dizzy and sweaty, with his tongue hanging out. Dawn's joy still reached him—one voice, faintly.

It's Fristeen, he realized. She wasn't just humming. She was singing, very softly and with all her heart.

Her voice trailed off.

"Are you there?"

"She's gone," Fristeen said.

Robbie took a breath and lay still.

A bird's trill reached him. Then a *lurp* from the pool.

"Is it okay to—" He sat up, and the leaves fell from his face.

Fristeen was standing a dozen feet away, naked, with her dress in her hands. She froze, returning his stare while a play of deep feelings—modesty, daring, whimsy and fear—flashed in her eyes. Then the strangest thing happened. The dress fell to her feet.

Robbie saw her smile at him, and she turned a full turn, one arm trailing, one raised.

It was Fristeen's dance of freedom. But this wasn't the same.

While she dressed, Robbie scanned the mossy hump and the sky above.

"Has anyone ever heard you . . . sing like that?"

Fristeen buttoned her front as she approached, shaking her head.

They had just started down from the rise, when he grabbed her arm.

"There's a path," he said, pointing.

You could see it winding through the reeds. It led away from the shore, into the black trees. They gave each other a long look, then they headed back around the Pool's rim, retracing their steps.

Robbie woke the next morning with a fullness in his chest. He dove between the curtains and threw the sash up. The sky was clear and the sun was blazing.

Breakfast was a breeze, and when he stepped outside, swallows streaked past, crying excitedly. The Hill was sighing and swaying, already faint with joy. Someone had swept a part of the deck, and in the clean spot was a word: "D-A-W-N," spelled with aspen twigs. Robbie sounded it out and smiled.

Fristeen was hiding in the shrubs. As he passed, she jumped up and hugged him.

"Can you feel her?" Fristeen beamed.

Robbie nodded and she whirled before him.

Something like a poncho rose from her shoulders, along with her skirt. Robbie laughed. She'd put two skirts on—one around her waist and one over her head.

They climbed the Hill, got the "all clear" from He Knows, bounced across the log bridge while the stream flashed beneath, and followed Where You Can See into the sky. Nothing hurried them. It had never been so hot, and they were glowing inside. Dawn's welcome poured like oil over everything they touched.

The Perfect Place was a sauna. They hugged and rolled in the grass, and as they lay there panting, a flock of chickadees lit in a fringe of birch. The birds buzzed and flitted right beside them, feeling their cheer and eager to join it.

Robbie lifted himself up and bent over Fristeen, shading her eyes and gazing into them. "You're so brave," he said.

The meeting with Dawn seemed like a miracle.

"I know why she came, Robbie."

"Really? Why?"

"She's tired of visiting when I'm all alone. She came because of you."

At that, the chickadees left their branches to roister over them, weaving an aureole of wings and song. They too were lovers of Dawn.

As they crossed Trickle, a frog hopped from the sedge. And there were rabbits, two of them, watching in the alders behind Used-to-Be. Nobody wanted to be left out.

When the Two-Tree came in sight, its twin crowns were flapping like flags. And then there it was—the land of secrets—spread out before them.

They hurried through the viburnum, Fristeen in the lead, and as they neared the first trees, her eagerness boiled over. She squealed and clutched her top, squirming inside it. Then she lifted her arms and pulled the skirt over her head, waving it around.

"Here," Fristeen said.

They halted beside the first black tree. Fristeen cast her skirt beneath it, then glanced over her shoulder at him, blushing. "Your shoes, you keep on. Everything else," she drew her breath, "you take off."

Robbie watched her slide the lower skirt down.

"Don't stare, silly."

"Why?" Robbie asked, removing his shirt.

"It's what you do in Too Far."

Robbie put his hands in the pockets of his pants.

"That's how Dawn and the Dream Man are," Fristeen added. She still had her back to him.

"Want some Cheerios?" Robbie brought his fists forward.

Fristeen gave an embarrassed laugh and turned, and he dropped them into her cupped hands.

They hopped through the pillows and followed the rill. Robbie felt strange at first. A branch scratched him, and some flies sniffed his rear. But it was great to feel the sun and the breeze—not just on your face, but all over. And running naked in the wild was a new kind of thrill that made Too Far even more secret. Their self-consciousness faded, and by the time they reached the Pool, it was gone.

"Look," Robbie cried, pushing through the reeds.

The dragonflies were back—dozens of them, zipping every which way, crossing the water or following the shore.

Fristeen drew beside him.

"They're the thoughts of the Dream Man," Robbie explained. "They come from his head."

"They're *crazy*." Her eyes darted.

The feverish flight paths knit a mercurial web.

They didn't speed up or slow down. All were going at full steam. One stopped, hovering with purpose. What did it want? Then suddenly it was somewhere else—just like a thought.

Robbie shuffled closer, water to his ankles, shoes sinking in muck.

"They move faster than your eyes," Fristeen said, right beside him.

In that respect too, they were just like thoughts. Even if you picked one and gave it all your attention, you couldn't hold on. You struggled behind, trying to keep it in sight.

"There," Fristeen whispered.

One had landed on a seedhead right in front of them.

Robbie drew an involuntary breath. The dragonfly's head ticked as the giant eyes fixed on something. Two bristling forelegs parted the seedy sheaf. Then the monster's face opened and plates slid apart, and from the sides of its mouth, two claws reached out, like some creature from outer space.

It gulped its prey and sped away.

They looked at each other.

"Strange thoughts the Dream Man's thinking," Fristeen muttered.

They scanned the far shore of the Pool.

"He's scary alright," Robbie said.

"Do you think he's here?" She raised her brows. "In the black trees?"

The challenge sparked between them. They shivered, clasped hands, and started around the Pool's rim.

When they reached the low mound, they searched the sedge till they found the path. And then they headed down it. Robbie led the way.

It was muddy and puddled, and it tacked without warning. You couldn't see past the next clump of willows. Robbie paused, turning, listening. When they reached the black trees, he stopped.

At their feet, a brave parnassia raised elegant white blooms. A lone spruce leaned over it, inviting them forward with leprous arms. They stood together, scanning the dark trail to where it disappeared, imagining who had passed there. And with what wild feelings, and what wild thoughts. Robbie glanced at Fristeen. Her arms prickled with goose bumps.

"Dare you," she whispered. "You first—"

He took a deep breath and stepped forward.

The path switched this way and that, skirted a seep, crossed a dip lined with coltsfoot, and then rose. The black trees leaned together, huddling close on either side. They were tall and thin, and lichen hung from their limbs.

"Robbie—"

Fristeen had stopped beside a tall spruce. It was covered with scales, but there was a place, rust-red, where a few had peeled off. She touched the raw spot and closed her eyes.

"It's thinking about *her*," she whispered.

Robbie nodded. "They came this way."

For a long moment, they stared at each other, testing their resolve.

"Dawn's our friend," Fristeen said. "But *he's scary*."

"He'll listen to me," Robbie said.

That seemed to settle it.

Robbie faced forward and they continued down the path.

A hundred yards farther, a wall of tree bones barred the way. You could see through it, but you couldn't pass. Then they realized that the tangle wrapped them on either side. Without knowing it, they had wandered into the Cage. Backtracking, they found a way around. A narrow gully reconnected with the trail.

From there, the way descended into a Hollow in the hills. A veil of cloud drew across the sun. The slopes grew steeper and the shade grew deeper, and the water that pooled here was black, not red. Something had happened to the black trees here—they were charred and armless. And the soil was barren—it too was charred, except where some affliction spread scarlet stains. Strange odors wafted from the puddles, sweet but sickish, and the things that grew here weren't flowers or grass. Mushrooms blotched purple; bloated boletes; fungus thumbs, slimy and white, without caps. The water looked tainted—oily rainbows swirled on the gleaming black.

"Fristeen," Robbie hissed.

He darted from the path, taking cover behind a spruce.

She scuttled after him.

"What?"

Robbie pointed.

In the depths of the Hollow, a dark blot appeared through the trees.

"See the wall?" Robbie whispered. "And the roof?"

The wall and roof were perfectly black.

"It's where they live," Fristeen said.

"Yep." Robbie scanned the woods on either side.

They listened. Silence. Stillness.

"C'mon," Robbie whispered.

He crept through the spruce beside the path. As they drew closer, a small cabin came into full view. Flames had charred it. But however severe the blaze might have been, the Cabin hadn't been destroyed. Dead spruce boughs lay curled on its roof, and a black lagoon was aproned around its front.

Robbie stopped. He bent and grabbed a rock.

Fristeen crouched beside him.

For a moment, he imagined the lagoon swimming in mist, while the roof of the black Cabin broke its surface, rising as if from a dream. He hurled the rock. It struck the Cabin wall with a *thunk*.

They waited, watching, listening.

Robbie drew himself up, and the two approached slowly. The trees around the Cabin were burnt the worst—most were shorter than a grownup. And behind the Cabin, in the bowl of the Hollow where the blaze had been hottest, the earth was ember-red. Fire moss flowed down the slopes to meet the lagoon, and as the breeze twitched its seedheads, the embers glittered.

The lagoon was shallow in places, and there were duckboards to follow. They crept over them in silence, seeing repellent things: creatures wriggling through the muck, or beneath, sending bubbles up; blooms swooning from thin stalks, anchored by pale roots twisting in the slime; or standing stiff in it, waxen and quivering.

The Cabin loomed before them. Where the flames had licked deep, the black logs were runneled and slick. In places, the beam ends had been gnawed to the frame. Twenty feet from the threshold they stopped. Should they try the door? Should they knock? Or just turn and race back?

There were smoky panes on either side of the door. Robbie pointed and they scrambled for the nearest, crouching in the weeds beside the blackened wall. It was blistering hot, and the breeze had vanished. The marsh vapors were thick and burned in their throats. They traded looks and rose together, shoulder to shoulder, peering over the sill.

Charred walls. A bed with a dark blanket. A brazier and a flue, and a pile of wood split for a fire.

"They're not home," Robbie whispered.

"Let's go in."

"It might be locked," he said.

But when he edged closer, he saw there was no lock on the door. Just a rope handle hanging from a black hole. Robbie put his hand against the door and pushed. It made a choking noise and swung open.

They peered inside. Then they crossed the threshold.

The interior was dim, and the smell of smoke was thick. To the right of the door was a small table, and on it—two bottles. Robbie picked one up, and Fristeen raised the other. The liquid in Robbie's was clear. Fristeen's had an amber hue. When they set the bottles down, they saw a large tawny feather. And lots of candles—fat ones, thin ones, short and tall—each with a puddle of wax at its base.

Fristeen picked up the feather and ran her finger over it. "Needles," she whispered.

Among the candles lay a clutch of Needle wands bristling with prickers.

"This is where they sleep." She replaced the feather and stepped toward the bed.

Candles lined a small shelf above it, and there were others, suspended in midair, hanging from the dark rafters on strings. Where the stovepipe met the roof, the planks had burnt through. You could see blue sky between them. Robbie ran his hand over the wall. The jagged char crunched beneath, and when he looked at his palm, it was streaked with black bars. He noticed an axe by the woodpile. The light from the window glinted on its blade.

"They have a trunk," Fristeen said. It was at the foot of the bed, and she was kneeling beside it, her hand on the lid.

"Better not."

She gave him an anxious look. "Should we wait for them?" She stood.

Everything about the Cabin seemed strange.

Then Robbie saw the eyes. "Look."

On the wall above the door was the head of a beast. Its long face gazed down, brown eyes staring. Its fur was singed from its neck to its ears, and its great basket of antlers was scorched and sooty.

"It's a moose," Fristeen said.

"Hands." Robbie held his own out, palms up, fingers curled like tines. "That's his name."

There were candle stubs affixed to Hands' points.

"I don't like him." Fristeen eyed the beast with mounting dread.

"Sh-sh-sh." Robbie listened. Was someone coming?

Fristeen was beside him, gripping his arm.

"We better go," he whispered.

They opened the door and slid out, closed it behind them, and hurried back over the duckboards and across the lagoon. Robbie saw clearly now where the fire had raged. It seemed a fitting end for the ragged spruce—maybe this was the fate of all the trees in Too Far. He glanced back, imagining the Hollow consumed by flames. Had the Dream Man been outside, watching? Or—

A squeal—the Cabin door opening. No, just an armless pole creaking in the wind.

They struck the path, and returned the way they came.

When they reached the Pool, they didn't linger, but circled it and headed back. Their clothes were where they left them.

They stopped at the Two-Tree to catch their breath. Robbie turned and scanned Too Far. You could see the Pool. But the path was lost in the trees, and the charred Cabin was sunk in its Hollow—from the Two-Tree, it couldn't be seen.

8

The rest of that day, they spent in the Great Place, talking about the Cabin and the Hollow, and what it all meant. It was nearly time for dinner when Robbie got home. Mom was in the kitchen.

"I'm back," he shouted, on his way to the bookcase. He pulled books out and thumbed the pages till he found what he wanted. Then, as he examined the photos, he stepped toward the kitchen.

Mom was fixing dinner as usual, but she looked strange. She was wearing a shiny blouse, and a necklace with a metal thing dangling in front. Her pants were so tight, you could see the shape of her legs. And she had makeup on—lipstick the color of Jim's plastic car, and stuff around her eyes that made them look hard and dark.

"Mom?" Robbie showed her the page.

135

She eyed him suspiciously. "That's a moose."

"Yep."

"Well? What?" She took soup bowls from the cupboard.

"Have you ever seen one without legs or a body?"

"A trophy, you mean?" She laughed.

"What's that?"

"People kill moose—"

"Do they burn them?" He regarded her uncertainly.

"Mostly they shoot them. Put your book down and take these to the table."

"Shoot them?"

"With rifles. Robbie—"

He was studying the photo. "Some of them catch on fire."

"Put the book down, wash your hands, and help me set the table." She smiled to herself and began dishing food onto platters.

Robbie nodded and did as he was told. But he didn't like the way Mom looked, and he didn't think Dad would either.

At the sound of his car in the drive, Mom hurried to the door, and when it opened, she hugged him and gave him laughing looks. Dad took in her costume and laughed back, but he was tired and Robbie saw the indifference in his eyes.

"I remember that pendant," Dad told her, being polite.

Mom hurried to finish putting food on the table, shouting directions to Robbie and apologizing to Dad. Robbie glanced at him. Dad shrugged. Neither could make any sense of it.

Mom saved the strangest thing for last. When they sat down, she struck a match and lit the two candles on the table.

Then she drew the curtains and turned off the lights.

There was a long silence.

"I can't see my food," Robbie said finally.

Dad laughed.

Mom's lips widened. In the dim light, her face was like a mask—etched with emotion, but frozen. Robbie couldn't tell if she was smiling or not.

"It's romantic," she said lowly.

"I think it's stupid." Robbie glanced at Dad.

"A nice idea," Dad said with a conciliatory nod.

"Please—" Mom sighed.

"Really, I mean it."

"You see?" Mom turned her mask toward Robbie. In the flicker, the painted lips grinned, clown-like. They twisted, vengeful, almost malevolent.

"Felicia—" Dad's voice had a sharp edge.

Mom was still staring at Robbie. "Go to your room."

"He didn't mean anything," Dad said, bristling.

Robbie felt a chill settle over the table, and he was suddenly fearful. Why couldn't he keep quiet?

Mom rose slowly. She stood for a moment, her head lost in darkness. Then she clasped one of the candles and flung it at Dad. Next, she turned to the meal—casserole, soup, vegetables—grabbing one after the other and hurling the crockery to the floor. Dad rose in the midst of it, watching her rage and the crashing and splattering. But he didn't respond.

Robbie stared at the lone candle, seeing it flicker, shaking with dread. It was flat on top, like the Dream Man's head.

A sound from Mom, half-gasp, half-cry. Dad reached out and spoke in a sad voice. Mom responded, bitter and despairing.

But Robbie didn't hear what they said. The rushing noise had started up. The spoon by his hand came alive, wings jackknifing out. He recoiled with amazement as the giant bug lifted, glittering turquoise and lemon, and circled the table. All the spoons were dragonflies, Robbie realized, and the knives and forks, too. Without anyone knowing, they whirred their lace wings and came and went. He heard a bit more from Dad, a little of Mom, and then the rushing sound mounted, drowning them out. The furniture vanished, or rather Robbie realized it had never been there. They thought they were on firm ground, but they were really just floating. The table—it wasn't real, and neither was the food. It was all just pretend. The rushing was deafening now. The house was careening through space. And where the living room wall was, the great eye of the Dream Man was looking in. A billion dragonflies whirred, the glowing hurricane churned, a billion thoughts interwoven, and what was real and what was not was, moment-by-moment, decided in the depths of that mind. Robbie's world, his mom and his dad— Whatever happened was up to the Dream Man.

"A dream," the deep voice confirmed. "A bad one."

At some point, he heard a command. "Your room. Go to your room." Was it Dad or Mom? Or the voice of the Dream Man? Did he whisper that? Yes, it was definitely him. So

Robbie floated down the hall, shoes barely touching, and when he lay on his bed, he bobbed like his toy tug when Mom filled the tub. "Dream, Robbie, dream," the Dream Man said. He put his head under the pillow to blacken the night, and the Dream Man lifted him. Robbie drifted in oblivion for what seemed a long time.

An outburst jarred him from sleep—Mom and Dad. Their voices pulled him back.

"I'm trying," Dad insisted, but he sounded hopeless.

"You don't care a thing for me," Mom said between sobs.

Then the rushing roared up and the Dream Eye advanced, and it churned and devoured what remained of the house. At the back of his mind, Robbie was wondering, "Is it really that bad?" And the Dream Man answered, "You don't want to know." It was just him on his bed now, rising, weightless. And then his bed fell away, and he was on his belly, arms spread, headed toward that great vortex of light. Below—a bottomless void with a few winking stars.

I'm frightened, Robbie thought.

"As well you should be."

The gyre turned, drawing him closer. *Where am I going?*

"Into my mind."

Robbie twisted his hips and teetered his arms, trying to master the currents. But they were beyond his control. The furious rush sucked him, the eddy arched over, the living plait telescoped out.

A nightmare, Robbie thought, as the hurricane engulfed him.

"Bad dreams are things precious the soul fears it may lose."

The dragonfly hordes whirled around Robbie, a myriad thoughts flashing, forming chains and uncoupling, twisting and cross-linked and woven with Ys.

"Breathe, Robbie, breathe. I want you to see."

Robbie inhaled and a deep calm infused him. The glowing plait parted and Robbie dropped through. It was a memory, a moment, a tiny cove in the Dream Man's mind.

He was floating above the black trees, and the Dream Man was around him, in the form he'd first seen him—a billowing cloud. But now Robbie was inside. The cumulus was suffused with dragonfly glitter, fiery trails like threads of stray thought, and the vapor itself seemed to glide forward, imbued with purpose. Then the dark mass folded in on itself, turning dense and doughy, and it fell from around Robbie's shoulders like a heavy cloak.

There was a path through the black trees and it led to the Cabin. And the cloak settled onto it in the shape of a man—a black silhouette, naked with glints, with a head impossibly tall. He walked behind a woman, naked as well, and she had arms, not wings. And as they walked, the woman was singing, and the Dream Man was murmuring, "Dream, dream, dream, dream . . ."

When they reached the Cabin, the Dream Man stopped and gestured her forward. The woman turned and embraced him, and his silhouette changed. The borders of his body dissolved, while his arms reached forward and his head billowed like smoke. His hands came loose and inflated like antlers, and a beast's face grew down from them, furry and long.

The woman stepped to the door, and as she approached, it swung open. Hands entered before her and took his place on the wall. She lay on the mattress and drew the dark blanket over her. Then the Dream Man's head billowed hugely, surrounding the Cabin, and his thoughts stirred anew. Hundreds, thousands, monstrous eyes gleaming turquoise and lime, wings whirring, threads circling, their flight paths lighting the cloud from within. Billions now, more and more alive, the dragonfly gyre hissing and crackling—

Then, in an instant, dragonflies fired inward, a thousand bright darts, and the Cabin burst into flame.

Tapers rose up, gold and blood-orange, licking the windows. As they danced, they reached, overtopping the roof, giant tears with blue hearts, searching and meeting. A sharp cry from within, and then a long trailing moan.

"Dream, dream, dream," the flames chanted, feeding the cloud. And through the flames soared the moan, like an answer. The woman was burning, with pain and with bliss. Her pain, Hands watched over with an understanding eye. And her bliss rose to join the one she adored. Above the Cabin, wings of smoke were unfolding.

The woods were hushed, now thick with eyes—wild things staring with dreams in their minds, rapt and expectant as the augured rite mounted. "Dream, dream, dream," the flames chanted. And the Dream Man's deep whisper wove through it all. The Cabin grew black, and the trees nearby charred. And as the great wings spread and rose from the Hollow, every heart thrilled, knowing its master. For the deliverance of Dawn was the triumph of Too Far.

The tortured voice faded and the flames died down. The embers blinked and the eyes dispersed. And the woods and the Cabin were silent as before.

The Dream Man didn't wait. He led his love aloft, and he took Robbie, too. Time past or time present—who really knows. But the Dream Man, and the one he wished to wed, spent the night in his heavenly home. And Robbie was with them, and heard every word. Vows and endearments—meant for each other, or the ears of a child? Or for all who would join them? Who knows, who knows. It was late when they tired, Robbie curled between them. And the Dream Man sighed, kissed his temple and spoke. "Fear is the fire, soul is the smoke."

Death to a dream is waking. As the morning filtered into Robbie's room, his dream slowly died. He was leaving a place of great exhilaration, falling down a dark well. The whisper of the Dream Man trailed after him, incoherent, indistinct. And then it was gone, and Robbie felt his head on his pillow, a new day prying at his lids.

Someone was in his room, standing just inside the door. Was it Mom? Bleary, he saw her regarding him.

"I'm sorry." Mom stepped forward and kissed his cheek. "We both are."

Dad was behind her. He sighed and leaned over, and Robbie felt Dad stroke his hair.

He mumbled something, and sleep rolled back over him. What a surprise—that the house was still there, and that he was in it. He drifted on the border of waking and sleep, and then he stirred again.

Robbie yawned and sat up. The light through the curtains was blinding. He squinted, gaze wandering over the brain on his wall. Had his parents really been there, or had he imagined it? All that remained of his wild dream were vague impressions, trails of two dragonflies circling his bed. What was a brain, really? Just a head full of thoughts, waiting to be set free. It's the Dream Man they need.

That's what happened to Dawn. She wouldn't ever wake up. Her body was gone, and all the thoughts inside her had flown to him. Robbie imagined flocks of souls converging from all quarters, their smoky forms blinking as they crossed the gray heavens, headed for the Dream Man's whirling eye. The notion so energized him that he leaped out of bed, threw his door open and stepped down the hall.

As he entered the living room, a deep chill stole over him. Mom and Dad's anger and pain. It had claimed their house. If it could, it would take him as well.

Trudy was on the sofa, filing her nails.

He hurried back to his room and changed his clothes, eager to relate what had happened to Fristeen.

She was waiting for him in the shrubs. As soon as she saw him, she hunched over and clenched her fists. Then she was sobbing, distraught.

"What is it?"

"Grace," she said venomously. "Can you get me something to eat?"

Robbie saw the shame in her eyes. "Sure."

"There's no food," Fristeen said. "She forgot."

"Wait here."

Robbie got Trudy to make him two sandwiches. When he returned, Fristeen wolfed one down.

"Did you eat last night?"

She shook her head.

"I didn't either. Mom and Dad had a really bad fight."

Fristeen saw how upset he was. "Why do they do that?"

Robbie shrugged. "Mom started it." He sniffled. "That's a lie. It was me."

"What did you do?"

"Still hungry?" Robbie held out the second sandwich.

She took it and bit in.

"I made fun of her." Robbie felt his throat tighten.

"I bet you're sorry," Fristeen said.

Robbie nodded and wiped his nose.

They climbed the Hill, followed the Bendies, and scrambled under the Fallen Down Trees. Neither spoke. The trials in their separate homes returned, filling their minds, keeping

144

them dark and apart. But it didn't take the sun and the forest long. When they reached Where You Can See, the view and the breeze brought them close. Fristeen stopped where the Dot Trees started and gave him a hug.

"Guess what?" she said.

"What?"

"I had a dream last night. I'm pretty sure it's true." She combed her lip with her teeth. "Dawn came to get me. I thought we were friends, but I was wrong. She's my real mom."

"She'd be a good one." He smiled and they headed down.

"She can be both our moms," Fristeen said.

When they reached the Perfect Place, they joined hands and brushed shoulders as they walked. They paused before the hole in the Needle Patch, then Robbie knelt and started through it. The needles pricked them as always. Robbie stopped midway.

"Fristeen," he whispered.

"Yes?"

He tucked his chin and turned his head. He could see her out of the corner of his eye. "Here." He pointed at his bicep, showing where a needle had scratched.

She put her finger to her lips and touched his arm.

"Did you get one?" he asked.

"On my neck," she whispered.

"I had a dream last night, too," Robbie said.

"Tell me."

"I know what happened at the Cabin."

"Really?" Fristeen scooted closer.

"She burnt up," Robbie said.

"Burnt up?"

"Yep. That's what you do. If you want to be with him."

"What do you mean?"

"He turned her into smoke. That's what Dawn is now."

"Smoke?" She was trying to understand.

"Remember what you said? The Dream Man hurt her, but she liked it?"

"Yes, I remember."

"It's okay if your body goes away," Robbie said. "Bodies don't matter."

A wand with long prickers elbowed into the tunnel just ahead. Robbie sucked in his breath and drove his leg toward it, scourging his knee.

Fristeen cried out, unable to move or do anything to help. "Does it hurt?"

"Yep," Robbie laughed.

They scrambled out of the hole. As he rose, she lingered on her haunches, inspecting the wound. "It's a bird's foot." She put her finger in the blood and painted the figure on the back of her hand, smiling as only Fristeen could.

Robbie took her hand. Where should they go? Neither was really sure. Maybe a walk in the Great grove. Had Used-to-Be raised any fresh blooms? Before they knew it, they were beneath the Two-Tree.

"Want to?" Robbie said.

"Okay," Fristeen nodded. "But not to the Cabin."

And they started down. There was mystery and magic in the black trees.

146

They shed their clothes at the border, reached the Pool and mounted a hill to the left, striking a fresh path. The sun was hot, and the thrill of naked freedom spurred their abandon. They ran themselves breathless, shrieking and whirling through swales of feather moss, shaking their brains and their bones loose. Then, from a great distance, Dawn's song reached them, and that turned their joy crazy. Their faces twitched, their eyes rolled round, their limbs flexed and jerked like demonic puppets. And what came from their mouths was all gibberish and nonsense and irrepressible delight.

Fristeen collapsed, and Robbie beside her, and she called to Dawn in a jabbering swoon. Robbie felt feverish, his vision blurred, and the mound of cauliflower lichen beneath them started breathing, buoying them up. Fristeen sang with all her heart, the heat blazed fiercely, and the mound lost its mooring and began to turn.

Was it too much to hope for? Not at all— In a corner of the sky, the clouds curled to either side, and as Robbie added his pleas to Fristeen's, Dawn plunged through! She was rosy and golden, a million bright jewels set loose as she passed, a million bright voices singing together, an ocean of joy, welcoming as a warm bath.

Fristeen whimpered. Was she sad? No, her heart was welling at Dawn's arrival. She sang of gratitude and confidence, not just for herself, but for Robbie too. Thank you, Dawn, thank you. Oh thank you, thank you!

Dawn's wings pulsed loudly through the gasping wind. Between Robbie's quivering lids, through dazzled tears, he saw the blurred beats—splashes of peach, creamy scallops, streaks of red fox, rippling and soft. Her face resolved, white as a cloud, hair swept back, voice bursting over him, filling his ears. Love, boundless cheer, solace in sorrow. Dawn heard Fristeen's longing. She knew Robbie's heart without saying a word.

A swoop of wind caressed his cheek—the soft fingers of her wing. With Dawn, no one ever feels forgotten. No wonder the Dream Man loved her—

Beyond the bright song, Robbie heard a dark rushing. And the more intently he listened, the closer it came.

"The Dream Man," he shouted.

Of course. Dawn was his wife.

The rushing grew louder. The air trembled, and then the earth. The edge of a gray blanket drew into sight. And as Robbie watched, it advanced till it darkened half of the sky. On one side, Dawn hovering in the blue, blazing and singing. And on the other, leaden clouds surrounding the great whirling eye.

"Hear him?" Robbie asked.

The rushing crested, and then the Dream Man spoke.

"Fristeen? Glad to meet you." In one ear, the Dream Man had the voice of a young boy. But in the other, his voice was booming, deep and wise. "You know my bride. I dreamt of her endlessly. And now I've taken her. Exactly, my children, as I will take you."

The last he said gravely, and their hearts leaped in their chests. The eye drew nearer, the whir of dragonflies filling the Dream Man's side of the sky.

"Love," said the Dream Man, "is nourished by danger. Dawn knows."

On Dawn's side, agreeing voices sprinkled joyfully down.

"Is it true?" Fristeen wondered. "That you turned into smoke?"

Dawn's pale face drew closer, smiling. "Yes," she whispered. "Nothing but smoke."

As her wings stroked the air, sun flashed through her feathers.

"I gave up my body," Dawn said. "I took to the skies to find my dream. And when I found him, the smoke became light and song."

"She is your comfort," the Dream Man told Fristeen. "I am everything," his voice grew softer, "you don't know."

"Don't worry," Dawn assured her. "You're going to be okay."

"Can I see your face?" Robbie asked the Dream Man. "Your whole head?"

"You're looking down into it," the Dream Man said.

Robbie was stunned. He watched the hurricane iris giantly for his benefit. The dragonflies were moving too fast to see, the great eddy a vapor of whirring wings. The lip of the cauldron was the top of the Dream Man's head.

"If you reach out," the Dream Man whispered, "you can put your hands on the rim."

The lip glowed as the churning thoughts spilled over it. Robbie didn't dare.

"I brought our friend," the Dream Man said.

Something shifted in a cluster of spruce. As they watched, blackened antlers rose up. It was Hands, just as they'd seen him—his long head, his bony basket, a singed neck, and nothing more—rocking in the breeze, then tipping forward and floating toward them.

"Why is he here?" Fristeen objected.

The Dream Man laughed. "Watch this."

Hands settled beside Robbie, bowing, the front edge of his basket grazing the ground. The charred tines slipped beneath him. Their palms were warm, as if fresh from the fire, and they cradled him gently. Hands lifted him up. Robbie hung his feet over the front edge and held on tight, but there was nothing to fear. Hands moved with great care. Suddenly Robbie realized: it was Hands who had carried him in his dreams. He just hadn't seen him. He looked down, and there were Hands' kindly eyes, gazing up.

"He's right," Robbie smiled at Fristeen. "Hands is great."

Fristeen pouted, but then Dawn chimed in.

"He's my pet," she said fondly.

And that did the trick. "Well, okay," Fristeen said.

Robbie scooted onto Hands' right palm.

Then Hands dipped and scooped Fristeen up with his left.

"Look at this—" Robbie reached down and felt Hands' nose. "He doesn't mind." The breath from Hands' nostrils was thick and warm.

Fristeen giggled. "His fur smells like chocolate."

"Want to see more of Too Far?" the Dream Man asked.

Robbie looked at Fristeen, and they nodded as one. So the Dream Man showed them around. Hands carried them, and Dawn hovered above.

First, the Dream Man took them to the Slope of Webs. The black spindles were so close that there were webs between each. Hands set them both down and started them twirling, and they went through the webs like spinning tops, wrapping themselves in tingling silk. You'd giggle at first, and then you'd shriek, because you'd feel something creeping in your hair, or down your neck or on your knee. When they reached the Slope's bottom, the webs were ladders, and bridges you could walk across. The Dream Man showed them how, while Dawn and Hands kept watch.

Then they crossed a valley of lettuce lichen, and reached the Be Green Streams. Busy rivulets netted a hillock of feather moss, and they hissed and gushed to invite you in. You couldn't stand up—you rolled and wriggled in the cool flow. The water was clear, but the channels were lined with black gooey stuff, and you came out covered with it. That was the idea—you used it like glue. You plucked feathers from the hillock, and covered every inch of yourself. Too Far monsters, born from a dream—burly and growly, and completely green!

Then the day grew hotter, and the Dream Man led them still deeper into the Too Far maze. They chased some ducks and followed a porcupine, and he showed them the first berries at Cloudberry Glen.

"I don't have any markers," Robbie said.

The Dream Man laughed. "We won't get lost."

Then he took them to the Cook Some Fish place. It was on a hillock covered with straw-colored rods flattened in the grass. The Dream Man brought his cauldron close, and spilled some dragonflies over the lip. Flames rose where they landed, and Dawn beat some breeze on them and made them dance. "No," Fristeen shrieked, and they both clung to Hands' tines. But he shook them loose, rolling them onto the glowing rods, and they writhed there together, sweating and curling like fish on a grill.

Then Hands lifted them up, and they were airborne again. It was a wonderful ride. You could face forward and see where you were going, or turn and look down at Hands' furry head. His blunt nose quivered as it tasted the wind. He gazed across the hills as they drifted, and now and then he would glance up and you could see into his eyes. Fristeen spoke his name softly and stroked his ear. Hands made exploring even more of a thrill, and he did exactly what the Dream Man said.

The deep voice was always with them. When he was guiding, it was with confidence and command. When he meant to teach you, he knew a path through your thoughts, and found his way with ease. If you had a question, the Dream Man listened. He didn't coddle you, but he was patient. He gave you the answer slowly, making sure you understood.

And, of course, Dawn was there.

The last thing they did was the most exciting.

When they floated over it and looked down, neither Robbie nor Fristeen could tell what it was. It was roundish and the wind ruffled its top, and it was big—big as a car. Black trees with turrets surrounded it, and from the turrets gray jays made a terrible racket. It wasn't till Hands let them down, that they realized they were on the back of a giant bear. His fur was shaggy, and when he started lumbering you had to hold on tight. It was like being in the water, riding a large swell, or laying facedown on a dune of shifting sand. Dawn hovered close, fanning her wings—their naked bodies glowed as they slewed back and forth, and the oily skim from the Be Green Streams mixed with their sweat and made rainbows on their skin.

How long did they ride on the shaggy beast? Only Dawn and the Dream Man could say, because it was right there on his back that Robbie and Fristeen fell asleep. Their idols remained for a time, Dawn on one side of the sky, and the Dream Man on the other. Whispers crossed the heavens, things the godly couple meant no one else to hear.

After they departed, Hands watched over the children with pensive eyes.

⌒

As daylight waned, they woke. Hands was in the distance, but he remained in sight till they found their way back. The sun's oblique rays lit his fingertips, ringing his head with golden flames. Then the bony candelabra turned and was lost in the spruce.

At the border of Too Far, they noticed some berries on the viburnum. They went looking for more, and came upon a wet meadow they had never seen before. It was fun to slosh through it. You could splash each other, and hide and chase, and that's how they stumbled on the special place. It was a bed of moss about the size of your room, but it wasn't solid—it was springy—and when you jumped on it, it was like a trampoline. There was water beneath. They jumped and jumped till their legs gave out, and then they lay on their backs and made it bob with their rears. Fristeen named it Big Sponge, because that's what it was.

They were stepping back onto firm ground when Robbie saw the bird. It was lying motionless at the base of a broken willow. He picked it up, turned it over and showed Fristeen. Blood was crusted on its front, and its body was stiff.

"It's dead," Fristeen said. She stroked its wing.

Just then, a chill wind strafed the meadow.

"Shivers wants him," Robbie said.

Fristeen nodded.

"What should we do?"

She made a helpless face.

Robbie glanced around, then stooped to retrieve a fan of withered willow leaves. He rested the dead bird on the fan, and set the fan on the water beside Big Sponge. When he gave it a push, the tiny barge drifted through the reeds.

"That's what they did when King Arthur died," he said.

For a few moments, the willow fan bore the bird up, then it began to sink. They watched in silence as the water circled the little creature's beak. Then it was beneath the green surface, fading from view.

"He can't give himself to the Dream Man now," Robbie muttered. "It's too late."

Fristeen stared at the water. "That won't happen to us."

At the border of Too Far, they drew their clothes back on.

They paused at Used-to-Be, so Fristeen could twine co-mandra in her hair. As they descended to the Great Place, she stopped and turned.

"Where are they now?" she mused, gazing back.

"In the sky."

They lifted their faces and scanned the heavens together.

"And Hands?"

"He's in the Cabin. That's where he sleeps at night."

9

The dinner blow-up was behind them, and as if encouraged by that, the good weather persisted for five days. Then the sun disappeared, and by the end of the week, it was as if it had never existed. Rain came and went, but the mist was constant. It seemed to like Robbie's home. A thick ground fog stole around the small dwelling and entrenched itself like a white moat.

Robbie spent lots of time at Fristeen's house. He brought food that didn't need to be cooked—crackers, fruit, bread, carrots—things like that. One morning, he'd loaded a grocery bag and was making for the back door when Dad saw him.

"What's in the sack?"

"Lunch," Robbie said.

Dad stared at him. It was a lot of stuff. Just then, they both heard Mom coming down the hall. Dad nodded toward the back door, and turned to meet her. Robbie slipped out before she saw.

Mom and Dad weren't fighting, but the tension between them didn't go away. There was courtesy and forbearing, but no warmth or love. Mom was discouraged. It was like the cut on her hand. She thought it was getting better, but when she picked the scab off, the cut was still there, bleeding as bad as ever.

She decided to redo the kitchen cupboards, and Dad sawed shelves for her. One night they didn't go to sleep. Robbie found them in the garage the next morning, still working. What did that mean? Robbie guessed for a few days, and then he stopped trying.

When Sunday came, the house was quiet. Mom was writing in her journal, Dad was reading a book. Robbie was on the floor of his room, playing with his marbles. One of them had yellow swirls like the Dream Man's eye.

There was a knock on the door.

"Can I come in?" Dad asked.

"Sure."

Dad stepped through the door and closed it. He went to Robbie's window and looked out. "Rotten weather."

"Yep."

"What d'you think?" Dad said, still gazing through the window. "Should we go for a ride?"

Robbie stood. "Where?"

"I don't know." Dad turned to regard him. "We could drive along the Chena or up to the Dome."

Robbie shrugged. Dad was watching him, waiting.

"I wish your mom and I were happier together."

He saw the understanding in Dad's eyes. Robbie tried to speak, but the words caught in his throat. Then tears heaved up and he hugged Dad's middle. Dad stroked his temple while he cried.

"Things will change," Dad said.

He was speaking of their family. Did Robbie believe it? It was Dad's shirt his tears fell on, but the eye of the Dream Man was in his hand, and he was holding tight.

On Monday, the mist was still swirling, but there were breaks of clear sky and the rain had stopped. Robbie rose, looked out, and dressed quickly, determined to escape. Dad was already gone. Mom was still in her robe, drained and distracted. It was easy to slip out.

When he knocked on the door, Fristeen opened it. She was overjoyed to see him, but she stood in the gap, barring the way.

"Wait here," she whispered.

Then the door swung wide, and Grace appeared behind her with a glass of water in her hand.

"What's the secret?" Grace said. "Invite Robbie in."

Fristeen gave him a warning look.

As he entered, Grace knelt before him. "Let me see you."

The living room was hazy with smoke.

"She's high," Fristeen said.

"It's true," Grace said to Robbie. "High and wide— Open to everything— That's good, isn't it?" she asked him. "Better than being afraid and alone?" She glanced at Fristeen. "Love is easy for you. When you're older, you have to get high to remember—" She paused. "That purity, that freedom, that infallible trust—"

She faced Robbie, threw her arm around him and swept him up. "If I had one wish— I'd be six again, and have a friend like you." She hugged him tightly, spilling water down his back.

"Grace," Fristeen yelled.

"Don't worry," Grace assured her. "Robbie understands. Don't you?" She kissed his cheek and lowered him down. Then she set the glass of water on a small table.

Robbie felt dizzy. The sweet-smelling smoke made it hard to breathe.

"Let's go—" Fristeen eyed him narrowly.

"It's cold."

She nodded and ran for a jacket.

Grace motioned to him. "Robbie," she murmured. She sank to her knees again, sad eyes glistening, inviting him in. He went, gazing deeply, feeling a little sick all the same. She still seemed beautiful to him, like a pretty flower that had a bad smell.

"I mean well," Grace said.

Fristeen's scorn pained her. In the weeks past, it had gotten much worse. When Grace was home, Robbie was never sure how to act or what to say.

160

"My problem is—" Grace raised her hand.

Robbie felt her fingers on his cheek.

"I need some of your luck—" Tears brimmed in her eyes.

Robbie took a breath. He had something he wanted to say. "There's no—" He stopped himself, then plunged ahead. "There's no food here. Fristeen's hungry. You have to go to the store." There was anger and frustration in his voice.

Grace froze. She seemed puzzled, and then Robbie saw a wounded look in her eyes. She had been so defenseless with him. "That's easy for you to—" Abruptly, her consternation ceased. Her jaw gaped, and a gagging sound rose in her throat. Then she bowed her head, and her words fought through a sob. "You're right, you're right. Oh Robbie— I'm such a dolt— I should—" She nodded to herself, wiping her cheeks.

"Great." Robbie tried to keep the tremor out of his voice. Grace was lifting her head, and he forced himself to look in her eyes. "Can you do it today?"

"Yes, I promise."

"I'm ready," Fristeen said, emerging from her room.

"Take care of her," Grace told him. "I'll be back."

Fristeen eyed her mother dubiously. "Where are you going?"

"To get groceries." Grace smiled at Robbie. "And after that—" She sighed and stood. "I'm taking a vacation—" Her gaze found the window, and she eyed the dense woodland as if it was an impossible puzzle. "From all of this." She turned toward the glass of water on the table.

Robbie realized she had something in her hand.

"A long walk on a quiet beach," Grace said softly. She

opened her hand over the table, and a red capsule rolled beside the glass.

Robbie saw the contempt in Fristeen's face.

"Go on," Grace shooed her daughter. Then she looked at Robbie. "Oh, I see what you see," she said half to herself, half to Fristeen. "He's—" She was on the verge of tears again. "—a real man."

"Stop it!" Fristeen grabbed Robbie's arm to escort him to the door.

But Grace held Robbie back. "Thank your mother for the handouts." Her eyes were suddenly piercing, like a lynx Robbie had seen in a cage. "I know what she thinks."

"Mom didn't—"

But Grace wasn't listening. "She's wrong," she said. Her eyes swam with emotion, again locking Robbie with a desperate appeal. Finally, she relaxed her hold.

They hurried out the door.

Grace called after them, "Don't get wet."

Was Shivers waiting? It was his kind of day. There was sun on the Hill when they started up it, but at the top, a chill came into the air. At the Bendies, the wind gripped the trunks and shook them, and when they rose from beneath the Fallen Down Trees, a thick mist gathered round them and everything was consumed. They waited, and just when they were about to turn back, the fog thinned and the sun reappeared.

He Knows was noncommittal. "Maybe" and "Take care" was all they could get. There was calm till the Jigglies. Then the wind rose and cut them to the bone. By the time they reached Trickle, they were both shaking.

"Robbie?"

The slope ahead was ponded with mist.

"Doesn't look good," he said, weighing their chances. The sun was still visible. If it vanished, they could turn and race back. He started up the slope. Halfway to the Great Place, Shivers rolled in like the tide.

The mist rose to their chests. They could barely see their shoes. The broth was freezing, the woods grew muffled and still. They stood shivering, watching the whorls turning purposefully around them, seeing the currents divide and flow, before and behind, and to either side.

"Go away," Fristeen shouted.

They could hear Shivers sniffing through the bushes, scuttling over the leaves.

"Let's go back," Fristeen whispered.

Robbie shook his head. "The Safe Tree—"

"Oh speak up, will you," Shivers sighed. "It's your old friend."

A freezing wind blasted down the slope, leaving everything trembling in its wake. Robbie turned his face, and Fristeen ducked behind him.

"We're not your friends," Fristeen cried out. "We hate you."

The wind struck again, wedging between them. Robbie

lunged for Fristeen's arm, caught hold of it and struggled up the slope. The mist rumbled like a blanket sliding toward them, sculpted from beneath by hillocks and scrub. Drooping cheeks appeared, the feathered brow, the sagging nose. The place where Shivers' voice emerged was snagged by branches, and the wind sucked and blew through the stretching hole.

"Love, hate—" Shivers was indifferent. "It's time. You're mine."

His spectral face lifted from the slope like a mask.

"We belong to the Dream Man," Robbie told him.

The cloudy lips twisted. "Oh, I'm happy to share you." Shivers laughed. "What parts would he like?"

Robbie edged past, one hand gripping Fristeen.

"Maybe he'll offer something in trade?" Shivers turned to follow them, milky eyes bulging. "Dreams, perhaps? Pity. I don't need any of *those*."

"Our thoughts," Robbie muttered, "belong to him."

Shivers' eyes puckered in. "Your mind has no life of its own, you fool. When Shivers is done dining, there's nothing left."

"Can you see anything?" Fristeen's teeth began to chatter.

"Help us," Robbie pleaded, trying to conjure the Dream Man.

"He's out in the marsh, bagging dream ducks with Hands." Shivers cackled.

"You don't know—" Robbie groped forward. "You don't know, you don't know—"

164

"That bonghead— That self-righteous ass!" Shivers spat. "I know him too well. He doesn't care about you," he said acidly. "*Dreams* come first."

Suddenly, Fristeen's chattering was magnified a hundred-fold. A fierce chomping sounded behind them, ascending the slope.

"Robbie," she cried.

Before he could reply, the onslaught reached them, and they yelped and howled as a thick shower of hail pounded down.

"There—" Robbie caught sight of the Great Place.

They broke into a run, arms raised to protect their faces, slipping and stumbling on the rattling ice. Shivers whistled after them. "You're desperate little mites," he jeered. "Don't you have folks?"

The first of the Great trees towered before them, crowns thicker than ever, impossibly high. The pelting ceased, but Shivers had other tricks up his sleeve. Through a hole in the canopy, a thick fog descended, and as fast as they ran, Shivers kept alongside.

"Great balls of humus," he roared, laughing. "I've got you now!" He was an orb, then a swept wing crying, "oh-eee-oh-eee," then a corrugated sheet eeling through the trees.

Robbie was losing steam.

"The Safe Tree," Fristeen shouted.

Through his tears, Robbie saw it, and he threw himself forward. Shivers whirled out in front of him, exploding in his face, soggy jaws parting. The wind closed around him, mouthing him with toothless gums and a wet tongue.

"Don't stop," Shivers garbled. "I'm having too much fun."

They were here— Robbie fell to his knees and scrambled beneath the skirt of the Safe Tree, Fristeen right behind. Breathless, they drew against the trunk, huddling while Shivers convulsed outside.

Were they really safe? Their eyes met.

Shivers circled a few feet away, huffing and banging the poles of their tent.

He puled and raved, but he finally let up. "You belong to Shivers. Don't forget." He gave them his word before he left: "I'll chew slowly. No bolting. Any care life or the Dream Man has shorted you—count on me. Time, I promise you." He whirled and tacked through the Great trees with a lunatic whine. "Quality time."

They made it back to the Clearing without a mishap, and counted themselves lucky. They should never have ventured out. Grace kept her word—she went to the store. Fristeen was thankful for that. But things remained unsettled for both of them during the days that followed. Rain and fog, and Shivers in the forest. At Fristeen's house, Grace in a stupor more often than not. And at Robbie's, the freezing space between Mom and Dad.

And the Dream Man? He just stayed away. Robbie kept trying. He closed his eyes and spoke softly in the dark. He went down on his knees, like Grandma when she prayed. But night followed night without a reply. Fristeen had better luck with Dawn. She came when summoned, but only at midnight, and her voice was faint. "Robbie will make sure you don't get hurt," Dawn said.

Were their idols retreating? Had marriage changed them? Were they just too busy? Maybe Shivers was right.

Finally, after a week of fitful nights, in the gray hours Robbie heard the longed-for voice:

"What shade is to a tree, fear is to the free. The sun still shines. Your soul is still growing. The waking world is still your home."

No picture, no light. Just those cryptic words, filtered through baffles of dark oblivion. Was Robbie asleep or awake? He rose—or imagined he did—and went to his window. Through the smoky pane, Dawn's first colors were tingeing the sky. As he watched, a dim shadow drifted across it. The Dream Man—distant, so distant. But with Robbie in mind.

Two days later, the bad weather ended. Fristeen was waiting for Robbie in the shrubs. The expectation, the excitement was the same as always, but the desperation they shared was something new. They ran and scrambled all the way to the

Two-Tree, never thinking to stop, shrieking and howling to keep their agitation at bay. Today was the day. Their idols would return, they hoped. No—they knew.

At the edge of Too Far, they threw off their clothes. Robbie thought they should go straight to the Cabin. But the black place still spooked Fristeen, and she wanted instead to call Dawn from the low rise by the Pool. They circled the red water, climbed the mound, and lay down.

Fristeen tried with all her heart, but Dawn didn't hear.

Were they at the Cabin? Or anywhere near? Maybe Too Far was alone with its black trees.

"It's no use," Fristeen said.

Robbie's eyes were still closed. It was at that moment, he became conscious of another presence, directly above him. First, he heard its breath. Then he felt it on his chest, like a warm night wind full of prickling stars. Then he smelled its fur, smoky and leathery. Robbie opened his eyes and saw Hands gazing down. His nose was quivering, his antlers flared wide—just a head and neck regarding him with gentle brown eyes.

"Fristeen," Robbie whispered, sitting up. "Hands is here."

When Fristeen saw Hands, she was overjoyed. She ran to him, opened her arms and hugged his neck. Robbie stood close and stroked Hands' nose. It was soft and round, and his breath pulsed powerfully through tear-shaped nostrils. They could both see now how old Hands was. His front was cut and scarred, and crumbly at the edges. And his beard was thick and dusty. When his rubbery lips parted, he was missing a tooth.

"Is it lonely in the Cabin?" Fristeen asked.

Hands tipped his head toward her. He couldn't talk, but they could see his thoughts in his deep brown eyes. He wasn't thinking of himself—he was thinking of them. He knew why they were there, and how much they needed the Dream Man and Dawn. And he knew something else—something he'd learned from so many seasons and so many leavings. And that made him sigh.

Hands lowered his antlers.

"He's going to give us a ride," Robbie said.

Fristeen thought he meant to carry them to the Cabin. But Hands' gentle gaze calmed her. That wasn't what he wanted at all. They knew they could trust him, so they climbed over his tines and lay back on his palms. The sooty bone was etched with lines. "Maps," Robbie said, feeling the surface. Fristeen nodded. Then Hands rose and floated into the trees.

He took a twisty way through the labyrinth of spindles, and the farther they went, the hotter it got. A nimbus of gnats joined them. They were dizzy and sweating, and their pale bodies glowed. Hands moved with intent, and as the fever mounted, they both sensed something special in store.

"Robbie— It's Dawn—I can feel her!"

The very next moment, they emerged from a thicket and Fristeen cried out. Dawn, giant and alive, burst from the skies. Her great wings were pulsing, and through the gaps in her feathers and her loving eyes, golden sun poured. She was dazzling, blinding, singing with all her heart—on every side she brimmed the hillocks and flooded the ravines. It was all Dawn's joy, her special gladness—like a peach your face was buried in, and the juice everywhere, fragrant and sweet.

"Do you know what she's thinking?" Fristeen said.

They were hovering above a tall hill, and as Hands settled onto its top, Robbie saw Fristeen's face before him, bright as the sun, with Dawn's great pinions combing the blue on either side.

"You should be married," Dawn whispered, and the silence that followed crowded out every sound.

"We should," Robbie cried.

"Just like you," Fristeen agreed. "Will you show us how?"

"That's why I've come," Dawn replied.

And that's what they did.

Not the strange way Robbie and Fristeen had witnessed at the Pool. There was another way that was better for kids.

"Lay here," the deep voice of the Dream Man said.

It was like the blade of an axe splitting dry wood. Robbie turned, scanning the surging sky for his idol.

"Inside you," the Dream Man said.

It was true. Robbie could feel the dark brawn beneath his skin. And the whirling he felt? That was inside his head, now unnaturally tall—like a giant pickle jar with a screw-top lid.

"Lay here," the Dream Man repeated.

Beneath them was a pallet of cranberry sprigs. At its border, the steep flank of the hill went down and down.

"Together," Fristeen spoke with the authority of Dawn, as they slid from Hands' palms. The wind circled strangely.

Silent, hands clasped, they knelt and lay down.

"We thought you'd forgotten us," Robbie murmured.

The Dream Man seemed not to hear.

"Ready?" Dawn whispered.

"Yes," Fristeen replied.

"Hug," Dawn said.

They embraced, their sweating bodies pressed close.

"Hold on tight," the Dream Man warned. "Now roll your-selves over—"

They started to roll.

"Again, again—" the Dream Man directed.

"Can you feel it?" Dawn said. "The edge of the drop-off—"

"Roll! Keep rolling," the Dream Man boomed. "Hands—give them a push. Hold on tight!"

Suddenly the earth fell beneath them—they were roll-ing free, clutching each other, turning and turning, hanging on for dear life. Robbie felt his chest against hers, tummies thumping like drums, knocking knees and shoulders. They were tumbling and tumbling, rolling down and down, Dawn's gold pouring over them, while the Dream Man's thoughts went wild in his head. *Your joy is melting into Fristeen's, your heart is a stream meeting a river, your deepest feelings are finally free. All this is Dawn's doing. Now here is my part. This swarm of trapped thoughts? This great galaxy whirling? I'm going to open the jar. I'm going to take off your lid.*

Every thought Robbie had from his first day of life—every spark of idea, each star born in a dream—rising toward the rim now, seeking their freedom at the very same time! Then, then, in a single moment— The vessel opens and the thoughts explode! Released, they're weaving a new universe around the tumbling glow. One heart, one mind, boundless, heedless, tumbling out of control.

"This is the way," Dawn said softly, "life should be."

A great splash! They landed in a sea of gold—the one Dawn had poured out for them. Two children, dissolved in each other, now dissolved in her.

Robbie felt himself sinking. He couldn't breathe.

Then Hands' fingers scooped beneath him, and Fristeen was beside him, naked and glowing. Hands carried them back to the top of the hill and set them down on the pallet, where they fell asleep.

With oblivion came peace. Robbie felt Fristeen close. Now and then, her breath reached his ear, and there were caring voices that came and went. Finally, as the day reached its end and the air grew chill, one surfaced, louder than the rest.

"The waking world," the Dream Man said. "What is it really? Would you like to know? An island of doom in a tempest of fire. The war is raging on every side. Here, right now— Open your eyes."

With the Dream Man's words echoing in his ear, Robbie parted his lids, raised himself and looked around.

The declining sun had ignited a purple holocaust—an enormous shrine with flashing peaks and sheer palisades.

Hundreds of smaller pyres flanked it on the circling horizon, blazing copper and beet, in distant lands. They were everywhere, surrounding the enclave of man, each with a charred Cabin at its heart, raising souls to the Dream Man and Dawn.

Fristeen heard him stirring and knelt beside him. Her body was still glowing, but with softer hues, amber and rose.

"We belong with them," Fristeen said. "I don't want to go back."

But what choice did they have?

They started the return to the Pool. Hardly a word was spoken.

They were climbing the slope to the Two-Tree, when a cold mist drifted past.

"A wicked lie," a wheezy voice chided. "It's all an illusion— just ash and dust."

"Fristeen—" Robbie looked in her eyes and together they turned.

At the base of the purple shrine, a myriad windows had opened, and through each the long rays of Dawn reached out. One seemed meant for them, but it didn't touch their over-look. It fell short, stopping at the fold in Too Far directly be-low them—the Hollow where the Cabin rested in its bowl of embers.

Shivers was wrong, Robbie thought. It wasn't the realm of the Dream Man that was wicked and false. It was the other, to which they were returning. Only unfortunates abided in that forlorn place.

10

The next morning, Dad looked up as Robbie sat down for breakfast.

"What happened to *you*?" Dad wondered.

Robbie touched the scrape that crossed his cheek, and shrugged.

"His body's covered with bruises," Mom said.

Dad turned back to the mail in his lap. Robbie laughed to himself. He had married Fristeen, and that was that. Invitations weren't sent.

"How about a hike?" Dad set the mail aside.

Mom eyed him uncertainly.

"Robbie can show us his patch," Dad raised his head in the direction of the Hill. "Maybe we'll get a look at the bear you wrestled."

Robbie grinned.

175

"That's not funny."

"Come on, Felicia." Dad gave Mom a deferential look.

Robbie saw the tenderness in Dad's eyes. He was reaching out to her. Dad felt bad about what was happening.

"Yeah, come on, Mom."

Mom laughed.

It was strange having Mom and Dad invading secret ground. But they didn't go far. They ambled up the Hill and looked at the view from on top, and then Robbie showed them the Bendies and the Fallen Down Trees without revealing their real names.

"How long has it been?" Dad mused. He took Mom's hand.

She regarded him fondly.

"We used to wander around in the woods," Dad told Robbie. "Just like you. In California. Your mom could get pretty wild—"

Robbie expected Mom to object, but she didn't.

Beneath the litter, the fallen twigs cracked beneath Dad's heavy steps.

"It was a wonderful time," Mom said.

Robbie could see the pain in her eyes.

"We had an idea," Dad said. He acted like he was speaking to Robbie. "Everywhere we went, everything we did— It all fed this idea: that we could shed the parody of life we'd both grown up with. That we could find a truth—" Dad peered at Mom.

Mom glanced at Robbie, a tremulous smile dawning.

"A truth we could measure against big mountains and tall trees." Dad faced Mom. "And we would find it by looking deeply into wild things—the sky, the earth, our own nerves, the veins of leaves—"

"The eyes of our child," Mom murmured.

"And this truth," Dad said, "would be something we would never find in a suburb or on a city street. Remember?" The last he spoke softly.

Mom nodded. "Our cabin-in-the-wild," she said.

Just then a thrush whistled, and when they turned to look, the wind blew and all the leaves flashed, and the thrush flew away.

Dad pointed at a stand of yellowing birch. "The leaves are turning."

"Yearning, yearning, yearning . . ."

They'd reached He Knows.

"The dark and the cold." Mom eyed the fall color with dread.

"So old, so old, so old . . ."

Robbie could see the weariness in his parents' faces.

"Dreams slip away," Dad said. "If you let them."

"Forget them, forget them, forget them . . ."

Mom sighed. "Everything's changed."

"Late, late, too late, too late . . ."

"Dad, Mom—" Robbie felt helpless.

"Stop, stop, stop, stop . . ."

Dad reached the stream's edge. "Look at that," he said.

"Back, back, back, take them back . . ."

The rest of the day passed without note. Mom took Robbie to the school to get registered, and after that she wanted to buy him some clothes.

But that night, as soon as Robbie surrendered to sleep, Hands' palms slid beneath him and carried him off. The clouds were sighing, the wind was sighing, and Hands was sighing too. Through gaps in the billows, the black trees appeared, gliding beneath them. The rushing sound reached him, rose to a roar, and then the stormy sky opened, and the Dream Man was before him in all his glory. The rotating hordes filled the heavens with a luminous vortex, a billion thoughts, all racing wildly, an ocean of voices, untamed and unceasing—

Now's the chance, Robbie thought. *Ask him.*

"We want to stay here," he said. "With you and Dawn."

"Too Far is a way station," the Dream Man replied. "This forest is my greenhouse, Too Far—where I cut and trim."

Hands swooped down, and the Dream Man swooped with him, grazing the spruce tops, dipping into a deep swale where sickly trees leaned on either side. Where the swale narrowed, the soft mosses had been burnt away, and the trees were all armless, black poles arrayed round a Hollow with a bog at its rear. There was the charred Cabin huddled in the shadows, blackened logs gleaming, fallen boughs curled on its roof.

"My department, my lab. Where I strip bodies off." The Dream Man spoke without omen or haste. "What remains

178

goes with me—through the spectral tides, to the sunset lakes. Here, Robbie. Look."

As they hovered there, the Dream Man came closer. At the center of his eye, the thoughts were densest: a forge heaving with jeweled bodies and spouts of crushed wings. And out of this forge rose a smoky pane. When Robbie gazed through it, he was peering over the sill, and the Cabin was burning and Dawn was in flames. Her moan was her soul taking wing as the smoke twisted up—a dream, longed-for, fulfilled—now rising to join and be always with him.

"Just a place of departure," the Dream Man said. "Nothing more. See yourself here, son. You need to be sure."

The smoky pane flashed, and there Robbie was: naked and wondering beneath the dark blanket, watching Hands float through the roof and take his place on the wall.

"Fristeen—" he said.

And she appeared beside him, her hand clutching his.

"Will Hands come—"

"No. His job is here."

"Will we—"

"Hush," the Dream Man whispered. "Just lay still and listen. This is something to fear—the worst flesh can endure. I'm going to rain fire down— There's no way but this. You're only dreaming."

Robbie was trembling, his breath fogged the air. Or was it Hands' steaming nostrils or the logs on the grate? The brown eye was wild like never before, seeing, through their windings in the hills of Too Far, some other struggle. Hands knew what was coming—

"Now," said the Dream Man.

The roof was pierced by a myriad rods shooting down—arrows liquid and burning—shafts dripping gold, trailing feathers of flame. And they all drove through him, hissing and straight—a hundred giant needles and a torrent of pain. Shrieks in his ear, the fletch running wild—

Hands' fur was scorched, his nose raw and smoking. His antlers were glowing, the points aflame. His ancient eye raged. Robbie, through his agony, found it and reached for its strength. White-rimmed, crazed, thirsting for unimaginable things—thoughts no one knew about, or were afraid to think. It was the mind of the Dream Man in that bestial face. And Robbie—what remained of him—dangled on the thread of that gaze.

Beneath, the pierced bodies lay limp as sheets, while their flesh answered the arrows with scarlet spears. Bloody flames rising, hot and ready. All that yearning together was now rising into the mystery of dream. The grim time was past. Young hearts and black trees, an impossible maze— All that was over. He and Fristeen lived in the flames. And as sharp-tongued flames, they would find their own way.

"No," the voice whispered, hollow and low. "Hands is dead. Your flames are dying."

Robbie saw it was so. The brown eye was lifeless. The thread he hung from was about to break. And Fristeen—where was she? Suddenly, the Cabin upended and began to float.

But no—it was he who was lifting, and he was nothing but smoke. His mind was a wisp drawn this way and that, twisting and rising, a sheaf of scarves reaching up and out. And a thought became two, and then six and ten. Flesh was too rigid to permit their flight, but in the smoky web the thoughts came to life—they grew beads and jewels, giant eyes cyan and lime, and they sprouted see-through wings, like puzzles made of glass. The wings whirred, the thoughts glittered and darted, testing the limits of a strange new world.

This web, with all Robbie's thoughts in it, passed through the roof, and a fierce sky spread out. A vast purple velvet studded with stars, and in the center: clouds black and doomful with a glowing core. As the winds bore you closer, you could see the core turning—the eye of the Dream Man, powerful and knowing, watched you approach.

Alien scarves wove through him, finding gaps in his smoke. And he heard Fristeen's thoughts mixed with his own. Gladness he felt, tenderness and mirth—a joy full to bursting—then panic. Terror yanked them together, but the weave rode the wave, and exhilaration budded, and a bracing gust blew them up. Again, fear and relief—the relay continued as they rose—and the cauldron of dreams grew closer and closer.

Fristeen, Robbie thought. *Fristeen, oh Fristeen.* Together they felt the bounty of release. All their jewels had wings and they were rising together, inseparable at last. From a distance, the surround of torn clouds had seemed motionless. But now they saw how it writhed, and they heard it as

181

well—a great mass of souls, adrift, wandering, some apart, some alone. All had come to deliver their precious gifts, to release them at last to the master glow. Here it was: a vortex married to an endless dawn, and the hurricane never stopped, and the dream went on.

Only thoughts? Robbie wondered.

"Nothing more," the voice answered from its blinding cave. "Is this what you want?"

Robbie felt Fristeen beside him, still close, but once again divided. They were no longer rising. They were drifting aimlessly in the turbulent sky. The earth below was lost in darkness, and clouds were closing over the dwindling eye.

"At the Cabin," the deep voice said. "I'm waiting."

There was a next morning, and it came with a shock. Robbie opened his eyes, saw a curtain beyond his elbow and a ceiling above. At a distance—not so far, when he sat up—he could hear Dad talking.

Just a dream, he thought. A moment of relief. But something was wrong. He wanted to cry. Was he sad he'd come back? It was cruel of the Dream Man—to frighten him like that. He put on his clothes while he fought with his feelings. He thought of himself with Fristeen on that bed, burning up. In the world he'd awoken to, it seemed heroic. But he wasn't a hero, he was just a boy.

Robbie turned to face the giant brain on his wall. Just a dream. Fristeen knew nothing about it. Not a thing.

He stepped into the living room in a daze. Mom shuttled plates from the kitchen. Dad was stuffing things in his day-pack, about to leave.

"Don't go," Robbie said.

"Mmm?" Dad turned.

"I have to—"

"What?" Dad asked.

"Some cereal?" Mom spoke over her shoulder on her way back to the kitchen.

"I had a dream," Robbie started. "Sit down. Please."

"I'm late already," Dad shook his head.

"I just want to—"

"Can it wait?"

"There's a man who lives—where dreams come from—"

"Robbie—"

"Please." He grabbed Dad's wrist.

"I wish I could." Dad turned away.

"I mean it— Don't go, Dad. Don't go!" Robbie's voice cracked. He dug in his heels and tugged at Dad's arm with all his strength.

"Robbie—" Dad was angry.

"No," Robbie cried. "No, no!" He screamed and held on, and he wouldn't let go. The Dream Man, the Cabin— He was on that bed, turning to smoke—

"Good god—" Mom ran from the kitchen.

"No!" He was screaming, "No, no!" There were too many secrets—more than he could bear.

Dad dropped his pack. "He's hysterical—"

"What's wrong?" Mom rushed toward him.

Robbie crumpled and fell in a heap at their feet.

Mom bent, grabbing his shoulders. Dad knelt beside her.

Robbie barely saw them. He was in the Clearing with Fristeen, and she was joyous and whirling, her hands trailing. "Who cares?" she whispered, and as she turned, her hands opened, letting go. Robbie's hands did the same. The rigor left him, and his body went limp.

"Robbie?" Mom put her hand to his forehead.

Dad slid his palms beneath him. "Hot?"

Mom shook her head.

Dad lifted Robbie with both arms and laid him on the sofa.

Mom lowered herself and put her cheek on his chest. "Let's take him to the hosp—"

"Let him rest." Dad put his hand on Mom's shoulder.

Strange, Robbie thought. *They were like a family now.*

He remembered a moment when the three of them had stood on the deck that first winter, just after they'd moved into the house. They had coats on, and Mom and Dad were kissing. It was the middle of the day and you could see the stars.

He took a deep breath. "I'm okay," Robbie said.

"What did you want to tell me?" Dad asked him.

Robbie's lips parted, but nothing came out. It seemed unexplainable.

"I'm sorry," Dad said.

"Me too," Robbie mumbled.

"A little more rest, and we'll get you something to eat." Mom glanced at Dad, begging him to stay.

Robbie turned, facing the back cushion. "Okay," he said.

Later that day, he was with Fristeen. They sat together on the crest of Where You Can See, feeling the breeze.

"It hurts. A lot," Robbie said. "And you never come back."

Fristeen listened intently, twirling a stray lock. "The Cabin's so scary. Does it *have* to be *there*?"

"That's what he said." Robbie rubbed away a smudge of dirt on her cheek.

"You can't go without me."

"Nope."

They gazed in silence at the great puzzle of leaves. Pieces of viridian, olive and lime were fit into others of emerald and jade, each bordered with black where their edges touched. Here and there, a yellow piece had replaced a green.

"Dawn's happy there." Fristeen lifted her face to the sky.

Robbie did, too. It was the deepest of blues, without a cloud. The realm of their gods seemed remote and benign.

"Would you do it?" Fristeen wondered.

"I don't know. Would you?"

"One thing I'd really like," Fristeen laughed. "If you don't have a body, you don't need food."

⟋⟍

In the days that followed, they spoke of it often—the ordeal of fire, ascending the skies, how life would be with Dawn and the Dream Man after they'd arrived. But they didn't revisit the Cabin, and for a full week, they stayed away from Too Far.

Summer was ending, and the woods changed quickly. The Needle Patch yellowed, then Trickle and the slope beyond the log bridge. On the Hill, the currant stems turned crimson, their leaves splashed with butterscotch, while the aspens above went from lemon to rose. A few days later, the Perfect Place flashed pure gold. When the Jigglies changed, the air was pleased— they were easy to play, these flimsy yellow leaves, and they made the most delicate yellow music. Then the Bendies let go, and the leaves fell soft and fleshy, and when you lay in their bed, your calm was deep.

And there was an hour at the Great Place—ecstatic, unforgettable—when a great wind shook the mighty crowns and that unreachable world came showering down. All of a sudden— You were unprepared. Through the glitter you ran, a fortune scattering and only one chance to gather it. You shrieked, your arms flailed, but there was no way to catch them. Then breathless, Robbie collapsed with Fristeen beside him, and in her upraised eyes he saw the reflected cascade: leaves and more leaves, a fountain of Dawn from deep within her, just for him.

Early one morning, the two children sat facing each other in the Perfect Place. Fristeen was eating pretzels and cheese, and some fruit Robbie had brought. Her face looked thin and her hair was tangled. Her socks were dirty and there was a stain on her shirt.

"I want to see Dawn," she said.

"Okay." Robbie stood.

"Do you think she's with him? At the Cabin?" Fristeen frowned.

"We don't have to go there." Robbie reached for her hand.

Used-to-Be had changed—the crosses it nursed had turned purplish, and red berries spurted from the center of each. The Two-Tree still waved in the breeze, but new flags had been raised—one lemon, one peach. And then Too Far spread out before them. They were both glad to see it. Autumn was sad, like your home. But when you crossed the border and entered the black trees, all that ending vanished.

The weather was sultry. The heat was pierced with tingling gusts, and the spell of forgetfulness was as strong as ever. They shed their cares with their clothes, and headed for Big Sponge, where they jumped and jumped. A small hawk appeared, looping and coasting and screeching over them. Then the rill led them through the soft pillows, amber and mauve, lime and maroon. Gusts chafed the red Pool, and wavelets were running fast to shore. They circled the rim and mounted the low rise, and they lay down on the moss, and Fristeen tried to summon Dawn.

Again, Dawn didn't come.

Instead, Robbie heard the rushing from a long way off.

"The Dream Man," Robbie cried. But when he opened his eyes, the sky was blue. There were no roiling clouds and no cauldron of thoughts. Just a lone dragonfly hovering inches above his nose.

Was it him?

"We miss you," Robbie said.

"I've been busy," the deep voice replied.

"We want to be with you," Robbie assured him. "You and Dawn."

"But we're afraid," Fristeen chimed in. "Of the Cabin, and being burnt in the fire—"

They both sat up.

The dragonfly darted between them, wings whirring with feverish life.

"Dawn belongs to those who belong to her," the deep voice said. "And I—" The dragonfly zipped six feet in the air, then zipped down again, glaring at Robbie with alien eyes. "I have other places to go, other thoughts to think."

"Stay with us," Robbie begged him. "For a little while."

"Alright," the Dream Man said. "It happens I've got something to show you."

Robbie stood and so did Fristeen.

"Where's Hands?" Robbie wondered. "Don't we get to ride?"

"He's in the lab."

The Dream Man's voice was dark with meaning, and when Robbie looked in the direction of the Hollow, he saw a coil of smoke rising from the trees.

"Smells like broccoli," Robbie said.

The Dream Man laughed. They were still close.

"Follow me," the deep voice said. And the dragonfly darted through the black spruce.

Even though they went on foot, it was still a trail of mystery. "Look here, look there," the Dream Man whispered, and they were lost in his voice, thinking things they'd never thought, seeing things they'd never seen. The bushes in the swales were covered with berries, and they were midnight blue and safe to eat. There had never been berries that tasted so sweet. And when they crammed their mouths with them and stood on their heads, the berries popped all at once, filling their eyes with dark blue ink.

"Get down, get down." With their noses in the moss, a new world opened up. There were glades of tiny trees without branches or leaves, each with a shaker tipped at its top. If you said, "Shake loose some dreams," they all shook, and dreams sprinkled out. There were forests of tiny antlers with bowls raised to collect blessings from Dawn, and remembrances of her marriage—cream-colored candle drippings, upside down. Mushroom caps were everywhere—apricot, lavender, and hot fudge brown. The Dream Man showed them how, if you looked from beneath, each was a world free and complete, a great mountain floating above the earth.

But all these things were just by the way. Before long, the dragonfly was hovering over "Put-Your-Arm-In," which was the special place the Dream Man had in mind.

It was a hummock of loose cone scales, and it was punctured with holes—some shallow, some deep. You fixed on one—how far did it go? You didn't know until you put your arm in. Fristeen tried it first. She wasn't afraid. She picked a hole, felt with her fingers and slid her hand in to the wrist. Then she closed her eyes and leaned forward. Her arm disappeared to the shoulder.

"What do you feel?" Robbie asked.

"Is that your hand?"

"No!"

Fristeen giggled. "Fooling, silly." Her eyes were still closed. "See if you can."

So Robbie chose a hole, held his breath, and reached his arm in as far as it would go. It was cool and damp.

"You've got the idea," the Dream Man said. "Would you like it back?"

It was then Robbie realized what "Put-Your-Arm-In" was really about. The Dream Man was preparing them.

So they put their arms in, and then their legs. And

sometimes they came right out when you pulled. And some-times they didn't. They just disappeared. The Dream Man did that so you could see how it would feel. How it would be when you gave your body up. It was scary, but fun. When you had both your arms in, and your eyes closed tight, you imagined you were bodiless and floating, just smoke drifting across a stormy sky. And the Dream Man was with you, whispering close, like a finger in the soft mud of a Too Far pool, drawing out a runnel down which new thoughts would flow.

But he left without a word.

They were jabbering and gasping, and they opened their eyes and the Dream Man was gone.

They found the way back on their own.

Late that same night, Robbie was jerked from sleep. There was a choking sound, like a dog with something caught in its throat. He rose and opened his door. From his parents' bed-room, Mom's muffled voice reached him. Then the choking again— It was Dad, sobbing. Robbie listened until he couldn't bear it any longer. He lay back down and put his pillow over his head. "It's okay, Dad," he thought. "It's okay, it's okay."

Robbie didn't say a word to his parents the next morning. He thought he might not even tell Fristeen. But they kept nothing from each other, and he wanted to talk about it, so that's what he did.

"My dad was crying last night."

Fristeen nodded. "Grace cried when she ran out of love for Dada. It's like the fire in your stove when you run out of wood. It gets smaller and smaller, and you get colder and colder. That's what Grace said."

The heart of the forest was getting colder, too. Time was racing forward, and there was no holding it back. In the space of a few days, all the busy creatures vanished; the buzzing ceased and the woods grew silent.

It was during this quiet that things finally came undone.

Robbie and Fristeen had spent the first part of the day in Too Far, idling around the Pool. They talked about their gods and the Cabin. They dared each other, and made short forays down the path, but it didn't go beyond that. In the early afternoon, they retreated to the Jigglies, and when the light grew dim, Robbie escorted Fristeen home.

Grace wasn't there.

No sooner had they arrived than the rumble of a motorcycle sounded outside.

There was a rap on the door. They didn't answer, and the rapping turned into pounding.

"Guess who," Duane shouted. "Grace?"

More pounding. Fristeen and Robbie huddled in a corner.

The pounding stopped. A brief silence. Then a large rock shattered the living room window, and a black boot followed, shards flying across the room.

Duane climbed through the frame, glanced around, and saw them crouched on the floor. "Where's Grace?" he said.

"She's gone," Fristeen replied.

"Uh-huh." He smirked, swaying, clapping his hand to the wall to steady himself. "She's only around when she's out of dope. Hey!" He tromped through the living room, bumped into a floor lamp and swiped it aside. It struck the wall and went crashing to the floor.

Robbie shrank, holding Fristeen to him.

"Grace?" Duane yelled.

Robbie saw the rage in Fristeen's face. She rose, trembling.

Duane reeled into Grace's bedroom. "Where the hell—" They could hear drawers dropped and splintering, then a *pop*, and tinkling as the remains of a mirror fell to the floor.

Then Duane stumbled into Fristeen's room.

"Get out of there," she screamed, and she would have launched after him, but Robbie restrained her.

They heard a window and another mirror shatter, then they saw him through the doorway, holding a doll by the legs and swinging it like a club, toys flying and clattering around the small room.

"What a dump." Duane reappeared, surveying the damage. "My cell was nicer than this." Then he barged into the kitchen. They heard him open the refrigerator. Fristeen approached, dragging Robbie with her, and when she peered in, Duane had both hands on the refrigerator door. He gave a loud grunt and tugged, and the refrigerator swung out from the wall, screeched against the counter and thundered onto the floor.

Duane noticed a solitary pear on the counter and picked it up.

"That's ours," Fristeen cried.

Duane smiled and bit in.

"You think you're so great," Fristeen sneered.

Duane laughed and nodded.

"You know what Grace says about Duane?" Fristeen turned to Robbie. Her eyes were wild.

Duane stopped chewing.

Robbie circled Fristeen's waist with his arm.

"Duane's a joke in bed," she crowed.

Duane's eyes narrowed.

"Know what that means? A joke in—"

Robbie wrenched her back in time to evade Duane's lunge. The animals in the black jacket shrieked and snarled. Robbie stepped in front of Fristeen, shaking his head mutely at Duane to caution him away.

Duane scowled and stooped toward them, then seemed to think better. He straightened, flung the pear aside and lumbered toward the front door.

"A joke in bed!" Fristeen screamed after him.

"Suck my dick," Duane muttered. Then he stomped out.

They heard the motorcycle roar to life and fade down the drive.

The two children collapsed together. Robbie felt humiliated. Fristeen cried.

"I should've kicked his butt," he said.

Fristeen shook her head. "We could have died."

When they'd calmed down, they picked up the broken glass and put Fristeen's room back together. Then Robbie hurried home.

As it turned out, he was in the clear. Dinner hadn't been served yet, and Mom didn't say a thing about his late return. The night was uneventful. It was the next morning that things really went wrong.

Robbie slept deeply and was slow to wake. When he left his room, Mom was in the kitchen.

"Is Dad still here?"

Dad strolled down the hall, greeted Robbie with a smile, lifted him and kissed his temple.

Mom was watching out of the corner of her eye. She turned with a melancholy expression. "Are you going to eat with us?"

Dad shook his head.

"I can't take much more of this," Mom said.

"Felicia—"

"We're nothing to you."

"Stop it," Dad said.

"Please—" Mom softened, making a pitiful face.

Dad put his arm around her, but Robbie saw his gaze flicker.

"It's okay, Mom," Robbie said.

"Here's a surprise," Mom glared at him. "Dad's going to take you to the lab."

"He is?" Robbie saw Dad's expression turn dark.

"Today," Mom nodded. "Right now. You keep asking—"

Robbie frowned. "He's busy."

"I don't believe this," Dad said.

"If *I'm* not worth the time," she said angrily, "give it to *him*."

"What are you doing?" Dad stared back, at his limit.

"Leave us alone," Robbie shouted.

Mom's eyes got large and she pointed down the hall.

As Robbie trudged to his room, she let loose a fresh tirade. He closed the door behind him and paced from dresser to bed. She was driving Dad away.

"Well?" Mom shrieked through the walls.

"Go fuck yourself," Dad said.

"I may as well," she raged back. "No one else wants the job."

Robbie heard the front door slam.

He paced and paced. When he thought enough time had passed, he ventured out. He made a beeline for the back door.

"Where are you going?"

"Up the Hill." There was indignation in his voice.

"You think you know," Mom said lowly.

Robbie took a few more steps.

"I'm talking to you. Turn around! You might pay a little— This is unbelievable. You're no better than—"

"Suck my dick," Robbie muttered.

Mom's face froze. For a moment, Robbie thought that might have put things to rest, and he took another step toward the door.

Then Mom swept down, grappled his shoulder and dragged him to the sofa.

"Where did you get that?"

"What?

"What you just said."

"'Suck—'"

"*Where?*"

"I don't know. From Jim, I guess."

"Robbie!"

Mom was shaking. He'd never seen her that way.

"It was this guy—Duane."

"Duane?"

Robbie nodded. "He has a motorcycle."

Understanding dawned in Mom's face and her eyes turned hard.

Just then, there was a knock on the back door.

Mom guessed who it was. She stepped to the door and opened it.

"Can Robbie come out?" Fristeen asked.

There was a long pause.

"Can—"

"No, he can't," Mom said evenly. "It's not your fault, but your friendship is over. It's a shame—what your mother is doing. I'm glad I don't know the details. What's come home with Robbie is more than enough."

Fristeen burst into tears.

"Mom," Robbie shouted. He rose from the sofa.

"Robbie?" Fristeen cried out to him.

"Go home," Mom demanded.

"No, I won't!" Fristeen shrieked. "Robbie?"

He was behind Mom now, tugging at her. Mom wheeled and cuffed him across the chest. "In your room, young man. Now!"

When Mom struck him, Fristeen screamed, and she was still screaming. Mom grabbed her arm and dragged her across the deck. Robbie hurried after them. "Leave her alone," he cried.

Fristeen was kicking and squealing, swinging her arms, beating at Mom's shoulders, trying to reach her face, striking her again and again. Robbie hurled himself at Mom's rear, clutching her shirt, lurching her away from Fristeen.

"Let go," he yelled. "Let go, let go!"

When she felt him attacking her, something happened to Mom. Robbie gasped as Mom's elbow jabbed his belly, he heard Mom's shirt rip, and he had to struggle to breathe. Mom had Fristeen by both arms and was shaking her wildly. They were at the edge of the deck. Fristeen lashed out and drew blood from Mom's chin. And then Mom just went crazy, bellowing and swinging with all her strength, slapping Fristeen full in the face. The blow threw Fristeen into the weeds. Robbie was sobbing, teeth clenched, still clinging to a wing of Mom's shirt. She wheeled on him, furious, and jerked him back across the deck, into the house.

"You've wrecked everything!" He kicked and tugged, trying to tear himself loose. "I hate you, I hate you!" Mom's face twisted before him, and he swallowed his fear and raised his fist to her again.

Her arm quivered as she raised it, pointing toward his room.

But Robbie just whirled and bolted back out the door. Fristeen was gone, so he crouched in the grass. He expected Mom to come after him. The door remained open, but she stayed inside. He sat there, his frenzy fading, dark thoughts closing in.

A few minutes later, he saw Grace coming through the shrubs. Her jaw was set and her eyes were blazing.

"Where is that bitch?" she said, mounting the deck.

"You better not," Robbie warned.

"Don't you worry." Grace saw the back door was open. Instead of knocking, she just walked right in.

She closed the door behind her.

Robbie stood, expecting the worst. First he heard Grace yelling at Mom, and then Mom yelled back, and then they were shrieking at each other. And along with their voices, you could hear furniture grunting, and heavy things falling on the floor. One of them groaned—a chilling sound. Like when you're doubled up because someone socked you in the stomach.

Then everything was silent. Not a sound reached Robbie from the sealed house. He retreated to the edge of the Clearing and sat in the scrub, alone with his thoughts.

After a while, Grace left. She had a dazed look, and she was mumbling, trying to calm herself down. As she started along the path, Robbie heard her laugh. It was a Grace laugh, so there was no telling if it was rooted in cheer or defeat, or poised precariously somewhere between.

Robbie thought Mom would come and get him, but she didn't, so he sat there till sunset. When he heard the car in the drive, he knew Dad was home.

A few minutes later, Mom appeared at the back door.

"Robbie," she called.

He tramped to meet her. She had a large bandage on her arm, and a small one on her chin. He could see she was still eaten up with what he had said. Dad was waiting in the den, and Robbie expected a big scene. But Mom escorted him to his room, and she and Dad had time alone.

The day's incidents had tipped the balance. Robbie couldn't hear their words, but their voices were loud and hurtful. The friction waxed and waned, and continued into the night. Dinner was forgotten, and Robbie along with it. That had never happened before.

It started to rain and the house grew cold, and there was no one to light a fire in the stove. Robbie curled beneath his blankets and Shivers was with him.

"Nice work," Shivers wheezed.

Robbie trembled and shook, and then he began to cry.

"It's always you," Shivers laughed. "I'm the last to point the finger, heaven knows. But it's all your fault."

Robbie curled tighter, wondering how it would end.

"Don't trouble yourself," Shivers sniffed. "They'll be back together, and you'll be there with them. We're all one big family, remember? In the mold. Till then— Well, it's obvious, isn't it?"

The next morning, when Robbie opened his eyes, an arm was cradling him. A warm hand stroked his cheek.

"Mom?"

She lay beside him, and at the sign of his waking, she kissed his brow. There was a rusty spot where blood had soaked through the bandage on her chin. Her lids were red and swollen.

"I'm sorry," he said with all his heart. "For being so bad."

Mom shook her head, tears glazing her eyes. "You're the most wonderful son a mother ever had."

"Sure?" He felt queasy. Her wild emotion had frightened him badly.

"Robbie—"

"Mmm?"

"Your dad's left."

He heard the omen in her voice.

"I'm not sure he's coming back," Mom said. She took a breath. "It will be tough for us . . . for a while. We'll just have to wait and see."

He nodded.

She hugged him. Her Mom-scent was thick. Her breasts squished his chest.

11

The days that followed were an ordeal. More than anything, Robbie wanted to see Fristeen, but Mom stayed home from work and she was viciously watchful.

He thought she was occupied. He circled the living room, getting closer and closer to the back door. He put his hand on the knob.

"Robbie?" Mom was standing in the kitchen entry. "Forget that little girl."

Was Fristeen okay? Her shrieks and cries were still in his ears. He regretted he hadn't learned how to use the phone when he had the chance. But what good was the phone if Fristeen was hungry? Grace might be gone, and there might not be food.

Mom's emotional swings were alarming, and without Dad they were unmanageable. When she was suspicious or angry,

Robbie was afraid to be in the same room. When she was downhearted, he was afraid to leave her alone. What was going on with Dad? Mom didn't know, or she wouldn't say.

He heard her on the phone a couple of days after Dad left. She was in their bedroom, but the door was ajar.

"There has to be some way—" Mom sounded helpless.

Robbie listened to the silence.

"If I can," Mom said, "why can't you?"

More silence.

"I'm shocked. I'm ashamed. That's some sultan's fantasy."

When she hung up, Robbie crept away.

A few minutes later, Mom came to his room.

"I'm sorry—" Mom hugged him, falling to tears. "I'm so sorry, Robbie. You'll never know—"

He patted her, wanting to help.

"Forgive me." She gave him a miserable look. "You will, won't you? When you're older—" Her face crumpled. "I did the best I could."

The next day, they called Grandma. Robbie talked first, then Mom took the phone.

"He's been wonderful," she said. And then she got sad and told Grandma that Dad might not come back. "I've tried," she said with defeat. "We had a foundation, something to build on— That's me talking. No, Mom. Really— There's nothing more I can give him. I'm not what he wants."

Later that day, Robbie asked if he could wander up the Hill. Mom agreed, but she made him promise that he wouldn't go far and he wouldn't visit Fristeen.

"I can't be as hang-loose as your dad," she said with a pained expression. "It'll be harder for both of us. I'm not going to lock you up. I just want to make sure that we don't get into trouble."

Robbie thanked her and left.

As soon as he was out the door, he raced for the path. He was only fifty feet down it, when he heard Mom behind him. The rest of that day and the next, he was shut in his room. Mom brought food and left without speaking. There was always the window, but things were so bad between them, he didn't dare make it worse. When his confinement ended, he remained in his room. He'd draw or sort his marbles. Or he'd just turn the lights off and sit in the dark.

The days were blurry. At night, he slept fitfully, unable to settle in, and when he awoke, he came to the surface gasping for air. He prayed for the Dream Man to come, as he had in the past, but the Dream Man stayed away.

One night after dinner, the phone rang and it was Dad. Mom said a few words to him and handed the receiver over.

"Hello?"

"How's my boy?" Dad's voice was raspy, like he'd just woken up.

"Great," Robbie said. "Where—"

"I love you, son. I want you to know."

"Sure. Are you—"

"I'd like to see you, but— We don't want to upset your mom."

"She won't—"

"We're going to have plenty of time together. Don't worry. Alright?"

"Alright."

"You're almost a man," Dad said in a playful tone.

"Yep."

"We're a lot alike, Robbie. Freedom's important to you. Don't let anyone or anything take it away."

"I won't.

"Promise?"

"I promise."

"You're not going to forget me, are you?" Dad laughed.

Robbie shook his head dumbly.

Then Mom took the receiver back.

That night, Robbie felt sick. Sleep wouldn't come, and the sick feeling got worse and worse. A half dozen times he dragged himself to the toilet, certain he was going to throw up. But the problem wasn't in his stomach. It was in his chest. Something had torn there. He was bleeding inside, and the more he thought about it, the worse he bled. *Fristeen.* He really needed her.

He parted the curtains again and again. Finally, there was a small glow in the east. Dawn, maybe. A little mauve puddle with a splash of peach. He dressed, crept out the back, and bolted down the path till the roofline of her house came into view.

How long had it been? It seemed like forever. What if something had changed? But when he knocked, the door opened, and there was Fristeen. She had a blanket around her and when she spread her arms and wrapped him in it, the sick feeling just faded away.

"I've been lonely," she whimpered.

"Is Grace here?"

Fristeen shook her head with a worn expression. Shadows circled her eyes.

"Dad left," Robbie said.

They shared the bleak moment in silence.

"For good, I think." He managed to smile, unzipped his jacket and handed her a baked potato. "It's kind of rubbery. I had to hide it in my room."

"Have you seen the Dream Man?"

"Nope."

"I heard Dawn singing one night," Fristeen said. "I think she was saying goodbye." She took a bite out of the potato and shivered.

Robbie gestured her inside.

"It's cold," Fristeen warned him.

He followed her in. The living room was freezing. When he pointed at the window, Fristeen stared at it. Then they laughed and found some pillows, and Robbie filled the hole with them. They did the same thing in Fristeen's room. She finished her potato and dressed for the forest.

"Let's go," Robbie said. "As soon as my mom gets up, she'll come here."

Thankfully, it turned into a warm day, a memento of summer, marred only by He Knows' oracle and the unleaving trees. The early light was oblique. Instead of flashing against things, it seemed to enter them. Every leaf and berry and flitch of bark seemed to glow from within. They all spoke their hearts, as if they knew this was their last chance before the dark winter closed in.

The Bendies had surrendered the last of their leaves, and the shrubs beyond the Fallen Down Trees were bare. But He Knows was waiting, and his squinting eye glinted. They needed him now to know what was in store, and of course he did.

"What can we do?" Robbie asked.

"Two . . . You are two . . . two . . . two . . ." The arching willow boughs seemed to have sagged, wrinkling his brow.

"We want to be free," Robbie told him.

"Agree . . . agree . . ."

Robbie glanced at Fristeen.

She smiled. Whatever they did, they would do together.

"I can't be with Fristeen. That's what Mom said."

"End . . . It's the end . . . the end . . . the end . . ."

From He Knows' narrowed eye, a spray of dark branches rayed like crow's-feet, things near and far shifting within.

Fristeen shook her head. "There's some place we can go—"

"No . . . no . . ."

"The Hiding Hole—"

"Find you . . . they'll find you . . ."

"Please, please," Robbie said. "Tell us a way."

"Away . . . away . . . You're going away."

A breeze passed downstream, a weary sigh. He Knows was finished.

Robbie gazed at Fristeen, and they stood there wondering. Then they turned away from He Knows and followed the bank of the stream without speaking. Dawn and the Dream Man were lost to them. And the sanctuary the forest had granted them seemed about to end.

They crossed the log bridge, passed between the stumps, and climbed Where You Can See into a clear blue sky. The vista was different—a yellowing patchwork with red and orange streaks. But it still inspired you: on either side, your gaze wandered the treetops, while your thoughts grew lofty from the breathless height. Robbie squeezed Fristeen's hand. She saw the energy in his eyes and drew close. The wind whipped her hair around them both.

The Dot Trees were leafless, and the Perfect Place was brown. But the Needle Patch welcomed them, eager to prick; and the Jigglies still jiggled; and despite all the leaves that they'd cast to the ground, the magnificent Great trees still had their crowns. They climbed the slope to the Two-Tree, a skeleton now, and when they gazed down, the secret land opened before them.

They descended slowly, savoring the quiet, feeling the spell of Too Far stealing over them. At the border, they paused where they usually disrobed. It was still chilly, so they kept their clothes on. Then they followed the rill through the pillows.

The reeds were parched and the dragonflies were gone. But the red Pool's magic was undiminished. They stood side by side for a moment, hands clasped, paying homage to their reflection: Robbie and Fristeen in the domain of sky and cloud, framed by black trees upside down.

"What's this?" Robbie muttered. He drew something out of his pocket. It was the marble with yellow swirls, the one that reminded him of the Dream Man's eye. Without thinking, he flung his hand back and tossed it. The surface dimpled and rings spread out to the limits of the Pool. It was easy to imagine some big finger had stirred it.

"Do you want to try?" Robbie eyed the far shore.

Fristeen sighed and shook her head. It would just make them unhappy. "She's with some other kids now."

Robbie nodded. "They've got other fish to fry."

Fristeen scooped her hand through the water, and took a sip. Robbie did the same. Then they skirted the Pool and struck yet another trail through the hills—all slogs and dead ends, but a magic labyrinth to them. They found a swale with dying plants that reached to their knees, and the plants didn't have branches or leaves, just long pale threads raying from the stalks. Like silver jewels, beads of dew clung to each thread, and as they passed through, the jewels shook off. A shimmering mist grew around them, and as Fristeen walked ahead with her arms spread, she seemed to float through it like a fairy through a fog.

They found some low hummocks, and they rolled down a small one with all their clothes on. A gentle roll, and slowly. But it reminded them they were married, and that made it worth getting soaked. Then they lay on the hummock's top and fiddled with the plants.

"Let's pick some." Fristeen lifted a vermilion cranberry shoot.

Robbie yanked a sprig of rouged blueberry from the soil.

"Put them in your pocket. Look—"

Maroon sphagnum tufts. Creamy lettuce lichen. And there—a patch of foxtails with magenta-gold sheaves. Robbie drew a pair of tassels through Fristeen's hair, and the aureole of filaments made her the sun she longed to be.

"I love it here," Fristeen said.

Then the sun rose higher and dried them out.

They skirted a marsh and reached an egg-shaped pond where two grebes watched them and spoke in hushed tones. When they pushed through the sedge, a mob of fritillaries burst from a remnant bloom, whirling around them, celebrating their devotion in a silent tongue. Cinquefoil seedheads, purple and brave; crossbills in the cones, going crazy, while they danced below in the rain of scales; a runnel where spindly reflections made ripples, inviting them into its hypnotic mesh; a bed of white cottongrass where they cried and squeezed, and watched the soft tufts fly away on the breeze.

In the late afternoon, they found their way back to the Pool. When they reached it, their mood grew grave. They stood for a while, gazing at the red water. Foolish games—was that all that was left for them? Where were their gods? The wind hissed at the reeds through set teeth. A hundred tongues fished from the verge and slapped the mud. The Pool was restive, and they both knew why.

Robbie nodded at the low mound on the far shore. Together they scanned the path to where it disappeared in the trees.

"Maybe we should," Fristeen murmured.

Robbie swallowed. Neither of them could bear the thought of returning home.

"Do you think they're still there?" he wondered.

"Let's take a look."

Robbie saw the dare in her eyes. He drew a deep breath, trying to steel himself. Then they started around the rim.

A breeze blew from behind them. Robbie felt the goose bumps on his neck and arms. When they rose onto the mound, it seemed like a stage, and Too Far was a giant lab, like the Dream Man had said, looming around them. Eyes were watching, like those that had watched from the Hiding Hole's rim. Eager, expectant eyes, full of dark rejoicing. Fristeen was looking at him. She was really scared.

Without a word, Robbie moved through the sedge, heading toward the path. Then their feet were on it, and they were stepping quietly along.

A cry made them jump—a gray jay calling from a nearby spruce. The arched rasp warned of something dire. The path entered the dark forest just ahead. The black trees leaned on either side, scabrous limbs bent, hung with hoary skeins.

"They're probably gone," Robbie said. He came to a halt, staring at the next bend in the path. Fristeen drew beside him.

"What about Hands? He could find them for us."

Robbie closed his eyes, seeing the picture the Dream Man had painted in his mind. He and Fristeen were twisting in agony, burning alive. Bodies crumbling to ash. "You don't ever come back," he said weakly.

"We wouldn't really do it," Fristeen whispered. "Would we?"

Robbie shook his head. "I'm too afraid." He gazed into her eyes.

Fristeen was trembling.

"What's going to happen to us?" She started to cry.

Robbie embraced her. "Please—" He felt a welling in his chest. "Please, don't—" Now he was crying.

"Something really bad," Fristeen said with despair.

"Maybe—" He drew a quavering breath. "Maybe things will change." The hollow words shamed him. What could he do?

Through his tears, he saw the sun was low in the sky. He thought about Mom. She was going to kill him.

"We better go back."

They returned along the trail, circled the Pool, and followed the rill toward the border of Too Far.

"Robbie—" Fristeen tugged his arm. "Can we see Big Sponge?"

It seemed like some jumping might brighten their spirits, so they took the detour through the viburnums. Big Sponge was springy as ever, and they bounced and reached and giggled and shrieked, and reached still higher. And it was working, they were both feeling much better. Then Fristeen dropped through.

All of a sudden, the moss opened up, and instead of flexing, her legs plunged straight down. Robbie fell to his knees on the bobbing mattress and grabbed her arm, and she got hold of the edge. She was frightened, but when she realized she wasn't sinking, she laughed, and he did too. She tried to boost herself back onto Big Sponge, with Robbie pulling, but as soon as she got partway out, the edge of the mattress started to sink. First it was six inches under, and then a foot, and Robbie was going to fall in, so Fristeen let go.

"Robbie," she gasped, sliding back in the water.

He was still holding onto her hand. Her head was just above the surface.

"It's warm around my chest," Fristeen said. "But it's cold below."

"Try again," Robbie said.

Again he pulled, and she tried to boost herself onto the mattress. Again it sank as she put her weight on it. Again, Robbie nearly joined her, and again she was forced to let go.

"My feet are freezing," Fristeen moaned, clinging desperately to him, struggling to stay afloat.

"Hang onto the edge," Robbie said. He freed her hand from his, set it on the moss, and backed across Big Sponge.

"Robbie—"

He leaped onto the bank and scrambled along it to where the willow stubs formed a strand. They were biscuit-colored now, stiff and dry. "Here! Over here, Fristeen." He started along the strand, hanging onto the dead stubs, slipping on their wobbling roots, trying to keep himself from plunging into the bog. Fristeen saw him and started edging along Big Sponge toward him.

"That's it," Robbie hissed. His feet were slipping, his arms shook. The willow stubs cracked as his weight shifted and he clutched at others, trying to hang on.

"I can't feel my feet," Fristeen moaned. "It's Shivers—"

"You're almost there," Robbie said, balancing at the end of the strand. "Can you reach that plant?"

Still clinging to Big Sponge, Fristeen eyed a tuft of sweet gale and lunged. It came away in her hand and she sank, her head vanishing beneath the surface. She came up choking, eyes wild.

"Grab my hand," Robbie cried, reaching, the willow boughs snapping beneath him.

"I can't! It's Shivers—" Fristeen was panicked. "He's holding onto my legs!"

Robbie swung out and hooked her arm with his own, expecting the willows to break any moment, pulling Fristeen out of Shivers' clutches, up onto the strand. The branches cracked all around them, but somehow they held. Fristeen hung panting beside him, shuddering and drenched, whimpering with pain. There was blood on her face.

Robbie led the way back along the strand. Breathless and shaken, they hurried through the viburnums and climbed the slope to the Two-Tree without a word. At the top, they clung to each other, clasped hands and continued down.

When they reached Used-to-Be, Robbie stopped.

Fristeen looked wretched. Her face was streaked with blood.

She saw his concern and she raised her hands, feeling with her fingers. The broken stubs of the willow had cut her, and she winced as she found the open wounds. At the corner of her left eye was a gash, and there was a larger one below her right cheek. A crescent cut crossed her nose, and a flap of flesh had lifted.

"We should clean them," Robbie said.

He found some damp sphagnum behind Used-to-Be, and used a wad of it to mop the cuts.

"She's not protecting us anymore," Fristeen murmured.

"This one's not bleeding," Robbie said.

"I'm so sad."

"She didn't know," Robbie said. "She was somewhere else." Then he had that awful feeling again—that sickness in his chest. He was looking at Fristeen's face, and the sickness was coming back. All the joy that had its source there— They weren't like the Needle scratches that would be gone the next day. These cuts were deep. And this pain—you couldn't kiss it away.

Suddenly, trills and twitters filled the branches. A flock of chickadees examined them, calling excitedly—sorry, caring, or just curious—it was hard to tell. It helped, a little. Fristeen smiled, and when the flock drifted through the branches, she peered after them.

"Can we?"

Robbie nodded, and she led the way.

To Used-to-Be's right, the fireweed had all gone to seed, and the way lay open. It was a place they'd never been. They ascended a low rise and a stand of birch appeared, barren and bony, trunks chalk-white. They stepped among them and Robbie put his hand on one. It was cool to the touch. When he looked at his fingers, they were covered with white powder.

"They're coming apart," Fristeen said.

Everywhere you looked, the trees were tattered.

"The Peeling Place." Robbie tore loose a scroll of papery skin.

The chickadees seemed to know it well. They tseeked to each other as they wandered through the ghostly grove, coming to rest in the crown of a big birch with a slash across its front.

"Look," Fristeen pointed.

"It's feeling like we do," Robbie said.

"Let's sit there."

They could see the deep wound as they approached—the bark was jagged on either side, and down in it, the brown heartwood was seeping.

So they sat beneath the Hurt Tree, arms linked, holding each other close.

It got colder. Robbie thought of Shivers, and of what life would be like without Fristeen. For a moment, Mom's winter dread infected him. He imagined he lived in a world of darkness, that all the bright growing things had vanished forever, and the joys he'd known that summer would never come again.

"Robbie—" Fristeen's eyes searched his. "We're going to stay married, aren't we? Your mom—" She caught her breath.

"Mom doesn't matter."

"Sometimes I think—" Her voice was despairing.

"What?"

"I'm not like Dawn," Fristeen said. "I want to be sunny, but when bad things happen—" She started to cry. "Robbie—" She shook her head. "My light's going out."

Her words pierced him, but gazing into those eyes he knew so well, he could do nothing but smile.

She frowned, then laughed.

The chickadees trilled and the Hurt Tree braced them. Robbie just smiled, and Fristeen understood. You could hurt badly, and still be glad to be alive. Fristeen's face—it was as beautiful as ever. Each cut was like a pair of tiny lips. And that great sun inside her— It might be sputtering, but it would never go out. They would always be together.

She put her head in his lap, and he held her with both arms, and they listened to the chickadees while the light leeched away.

It was as Robbie expected. He could see Mom's silhouette in the window as they reached the bottom of the Hill. Fristeen

218

hurried through the shrubs. When he was halfway across the deck, the back door flew open and Mom rushed out.

"Why, Robbie? Why? Why? Why?"

She dragged him across the living room and they fell together on the floor.

"Answer me," Mom shrieked.

Robbie couldn't find his voice.

"Answer me!" Mom shook her head savagely, and then her lips puffed out and she was bawling miserably, falling apart.

"Mom—" He just stared at her. "Mom—" Why wasn't Dad here? He would know what to do.

"I'm sorry, I'm sorry," Mom struggled with her breath. "I'm overreacting—"

Something terrible is happening, Robbie thought.

"I've quit." Mom closed her eyes to see her thoughts more clearly. "I've quit."

"Your job?"

She nodded, then broke again, sobbing quietly to herself.

"I had to see her," Robbie said. "I just had to." He slid his hand in his pocket the way Dad might do.

Mom shook her head. "It doesn't matter." She tried to smile. "It's over now."

Robbie's fingers felt the leaves. He didn't realize what they were till he drew them out. A sprig of rouged blueberry, creamy lettuce lichens and a pair of sphagnum rosettes with velvety stalks.

Mom's expression was quizzical, then she melted as he reached up and planted them in her hair. Fresh tears wet her cheeks, grateful tears.

"You're beautiful, Mom. We'll be okay."

"Yep," she blurted, and she laughed adoringly. "It will be easier— Once all this is behind us." She gazed around the sad house. "We're leaving," she said. "Going back to the States. Maybe Thursday—just a few days."

Robbie stared at her.

"I've started to pack." Mom kissed him. "We'll stay with Grandma. Till things make more sense. Did you cut yourself?" Mom frowned.

"No—"

"You've got blood on your hands."

〜

Sleep didn't come quickly, but by midnight, Robbie was deep in a dream.

He knew where he was—the Peeling Trees were all around him. The sky was dark gray, and he could hear distant rain. A pale ground fog covered everything to the level of his knees, and the trees rising above it were trembling, as if trying to uproot themselves. But none of them could move, and neither could he.

A familiar rumble rose through the woodland. A motorcycle and rider appeared, speeding toward him, wheels gliding smoothly beneath the blanket of fog. It's Duane, Robbie thought. But when the cycle roared up, spitting leaf litter and gravel, it was Grace who was straddling the growling machine. She shook her hair in the breeze, gave an exhilarated sigh, and regarded him with her sparkling eyes. She wore Duane's jacket, and she'd brought the rain with her. Robbie could hear the drops tapping on the hard leather, while the beady-eyed animals squeaked and snarled within.

"I heard you talking about him," Grace laughed. "I saw the target you tacked on the laundry room door."

"Shivers?"

"One night, he came to visit. And— I couldn't send him home." Grace eyed Robbie with deep emotion. "I knew it would happen. I told you—"

"What?" Robbie said numbly.

"My Romeo, dear. My Romeo!" Grace beamed, and held her hand up. "We're married now. See my ring?"

Her finger was cut clean around, and lumps of blood glittered in a band of white pus.

"I'm taking her away—" Shivers' voice rose from the fog.

Grace saw the recognition in Robbie's face. "You're old friends."

"He's a monster," Robbie told her. "He eats people. You can't go away."

Grace was surprised. "Why not?"

"You have to stay and take care of Fristeen."

Grace laughed. "*You're* doing *that*."

"He's almost a man," Shivers said acidly.

Suddenly, the ground fog was gathering, bunching before Robbie, drawing in from the borders of the grove. It billowed and towered, sucking air up, dripping and giving off odors of canker and mold. The lumpy brow mushroomed, the sagging nose pushed out, and deep in the dark eye holes, white balloons grew—shriveled at first, bulging as they filled with noxious gas. His chin lay coiled over an expanse of soaked moss.

"Nice job," Shivers wheezed. He cracked his chin to the side.

The moss was floating, and there was a gaping hole, like the hole at Big Sponge. On a giant fan of dead willow leaves, Fristeen lay floating, naked and stiff. Her eyes were open, frozen in mute despair, and around them the cuts from the willow stubs were crawling, bending and twisting like purple worms.

"She's doing just fine," Grace frowned. "Don't you think?"

Shivers nodded. "I like her *better* this way."

"Well," Grace smiled at Robbie. "It's almost over. You'll be along shortly?"

"Yes," Shivers said. "I'll be along."

With that, Grace revved the motorcycle and roared away through the trees.

Almost over, Robbie thought.

Then he realized that Fristeen's willow barge was sinking. The water crept over the crinkled wales and the stern went under, turning her ankles green. He cried out and fell to his

222

knees, trying to reach her, but his feet were like a tree's, rooted in the earth. Water poured into the barge now, swamping it completely, and Fristeen was sinking, her face gazing up at him. Robbie felt himself shuddering from head to foot. Was it the fog, or what he saw as the water closed over her? Fristeen was cold, joyless as a stone. Her likeness to Dawn was gone for good. The white mouth was around him now, and everything was mist. Shivers swallowed him whole, and began to chew.

The end . . . the end . . . Just like He Knows said.

Robbie's senses faded. He heard Shivers' juices, inexorably churning. And then another sound rose and obscured even that. A rushing, a rushing—

Could it be— Could it be—

Yes! A great rushing, not of the wind, not made of dead chill and Shivers, but of feverish life, joyous and frenzied, powerful enough to sweep all fears away.

The Dream Man was speaking!

"I'm here now, Robbie. Be calm.

"Why haven't I come? I'm impatient, covetous—sometimes I'm crazed. I plot and move on, my restless thoughts race. It's autumn—I scorch the forest in my haste. Raze it! Make it blaze! I will not wait. Yellow's my disdain for those left in my wake. Russet my regret, and gold my relief— For the passing dream, Robbie, puts an end to all. To be free, you see, means always leaving, or returning to the place where leaves never fall.

"Dream, Robbie. Dream. Put poor Shivers out."

All at once, the Dream Man's heaven seemed very close. Robbie could feel himself floating way up in the sky. He could hear the stars bursting to life, he could smell their sparks.

"Mysteries endless, wonders unceasing. No season of dying and no thought of return. A new life to lead, new air to breathe; a soul mixed with your own. Her name is Fristeen.

"Dream, Robbie. Dream. It's not too late."

The Dream Man was chanting a song of great romance, and they were its heroes, flying to meet him.

"You're a prince, born of thought, son of thought's king. And to thought you will return, unshackled and free. To me, my dear son. Be brave. Say goodbye."

They had been cleansed in the Cabin. They had risen in smoke. They had passed through the stormwind, and entered the cauldron. They'd been crushed and consumed with the Dream Man's thoughts. And now they floated in that bright place where he and Dawn had withdrawn to. Their home in the skies, where his power met her peace. Where ideas spanned the ether, fast as dragonflies, and joy poured out from an infinite source. Where the clouds made moods for you, and the winds made music, and a love pure, desiring a splendor sky-wide, pricked and painted itself with blood from a thousand horizons.

Robbie jerked upright, sheets in both fists, knowing what he would do.

He dressed quietly, opened his window and clambered over the sill.

12

The night was cold and clear. A silver glow lit the ground. Robbie hurried along the path to Fristeen's house. When he arrived, all the windows were dark. He rapped on the door. A moment later, it creaked open and Fristeen's pale face appeared in the gap, marked by dashes and squiggles, but otherwise intact.

He threw his arms around her, hugged her, then checked to make sure, gazing deeply, seeing the sun in her heart and the life in her eyes. She giggled and touched his nose with her finger. He was so happy, he could barely speak.

They stepped into the house together. It was very cold. Fristeen retrieved a branch from a small pile and faced him.

"Do you know how to make a fire in the stove?"

Robbie stared at her. "The Dream Man spoke to me."

She cocked her head.

"He still wants us," Robbie said.

"The Cabin?" Her eyes grew wide.

"Is Grace here?" He glanced toward the back.

Fristeen shook her head.

"It's our last chance," he said. "Mom's going to take me away."

"No." Fristeen dropped the branch. "She can't do that."

Robbie scowled. "It's hopeless here."

They locked gazes, thinking about the things that had happened. *Here* seemed to take in so very much.

"Let's go live with them." Fristeen quivered as she spoke.

"We have to go now, before Mom wakes up."

"Okay." And she went to dress.

"Put something warm on," he called after. "It's freezing outside."

Freezing and spooky. Every noise startled them—boughs scraping, something ticking in the scrub, their own feet crunching the leaves. As they approached the crest of the Hill, the moon rose over it, nearly full. Tall aspens were silhouetted on either side, their branching crowns once again leafless, like the nerve trees in the poster on Robbie's bedroom wall.

How far in the past all that seemed.

They topped the Hill, and the moon swung clear. Everything was in view, and they knew the way well. But the forest was very different in the dark. The Bendies loomed threateningly, the wind rat-tatted the weave of the Fallen Down Trees. Robbie walked past He Knows without stopping, and when

Fristeen objected, he shook his head. "It's *not* the end."

Was Shivers already with them? Their breath fogged the air. When they reached the twin stumps at the start of Where You Can See, Fristeen stopped.

"Can we have some soup?"

Robbie nodded. "It's ready." He held an invisible spoon to his lips and blew on it. Then he brought it toward her.

Fristeen took a sip. "Much better," she said.

But the biting wind on the high ridge was a true taste of winter, and the higher they climbed the more they shook. The view below, always jolting, was nearly obscure. The view above and beyond, was like nothing Robbie had ever seen. Beneath the moon, rows of cloudbanks were pearling—the backs of waves headed away from this world, into the next.

They descended through the Dot Trees, seeing a new magic—the dots glowed in the moonlight. All the branches were twisted with stars, and each time your eye shifted, a new Pleiades rose through the glittering web. But as the two of them approached the slope's bottom, the magic turned menacing. New stars were settling, falling out of the sky. The branches were glittering with snow.

"Shivers," Robbie muttered.

As if in response, the snow fell harder. Robbie felt Shivers' cold breath on his back. His toes began to ache and his fingers hurt. Fristeen made fists and held them beneath her chin. They faced into the wind and crossed the Perfect Place. The meadow was turning white. The wind beat against them and

227

whistled in their ears. Robbie blamed himself. Why had he been so fearful? They had so many chances to reach the Cabin when the sun was out.

He found the dark opening in the Needle Patch, and they squirmed through it as quickly as they could. But when they rose on the far side, the snow was falling fast and the way to the Jigglies was nothing but a guess. Robbie stumbled forward, arm raised, squinting to keep the drift from his eyes. The way grew dimmer. Shivers was curtaining the moon. What were those sighings, those wheezings nearby? The murky thickets hid invisible creatures, following, watching, pausing when they did, huddling to confer.

The white rods above them—they were Jigglies, weren't they? Robbie couldn't see the marker he'd left there, everything was so padded with white— Yes, the Jigglies. He was feeling his way, but he knew where he was. The snow's surface was deceptive. It looked perfectly smooth, but when you put your foot down, twigs crunched like bones. He wiggled his toes in his shoes. He could barely feel them.

"Are you okay?" Robbie glanced back.

Fristeen nodded. "I'm really cold. Is this the way?" She eyed the white thickets around them warily. Everything looked so strange.

The tangled web looked strange to him, too. Where was Trickle? Was it beneath the white blanket? Had he walked past it without knowing? He glanced back. The falling snow was filling their prints. He started forward, then stopped.

"Fristeen—" Robbie turned to her.

She saw the confusion in his face.

"We need to go back to the Patch," he said.

But when he tried to backtrack, what he thought was their trail led him to another place that looked unfamiliar. The cold snow was falling even more thickly, and a bucking wind was kicking the new drifts. When he stopped again, Fristeen linked arms with him, looking anxiously to either side. They both knew—they were lost.

A shrill wheeze rose behind them, and a sudden flurry consumed them. They hugged, hiding their faces from the whirling snow.

"Tonight's the night," Shivers whispered in Robbie's ear. The flurry shifted, swirling behind a rise, dragging a long chin behind. "A new beginning," Shivers promised. "Tonight . . . tonight . . ."

To the right, the ground tended up. Maybe he could find a high point, Robbie thought. If the snowfall thinned, he'd be able to see. He glanced at Fristeen and started to climb. She followed behind. The wind blew fiercely, the white cleared for a moment, and the Cage stood out from the slope. Robbie's hope rose. But they weren't in Too Far, and it wasn't the Cage—it was some other tangle with a great stump in the center, and as they struggled around it, something atop the stump shifted. It hunched in the wind and slid onto Robbie's shoulders like a heavy cape. He heard sucking sounds as he fought with it, and then a hooded head jutted from its mossy fringe. "A juicy spot," Shivers wheezed. "Relax and settle in." A stringy tongue darted through soggy lips, sagging nose dripping between cheeks loam brown. Fristeen grabbed hold, and together they threw the moss off.

Suddenly the snow gave way and they sank to their hips. A deadfall opened, gaping to swallow them, Shivers beneath them, mouthing eagerly. Robbie fought to get loose, sinking, panicked, Fristeen screaming in his ear. She churned beside him, scrambling and stumbling, dragging him with her out of the hole.

"Robbie—"

He clutched her.

"Touching," Shivers mewled. "Devotion, my sweets, is life's great farce. The heartwood molders the same as the bark."

"What do you know?" Fristeen lashed out.

"*You*," the wheezy voice twisted with hatred, "are snot in Shivers' nose."

In his mind, Robbie reached for the Dream Man. *Please,* he begged. *I need your help.*

He grabbed Fristeen's hand and started to move again, forcing his way through the furious blast. Trunks cracked, branches hurled, whole trees tumbled past. Shivers was tearing up the forest around them. Robbie sank to his knees in drifted snow. Where was he going? Should they stop and huddle down? Try to get warm? Shivers saw his weakness and swept up behind him. Robbie heard throaty breathing, and when he turned, a flying branch struck him in the face.

Fristeen screamed.

Robbie buckled with pain, sharp things in his mouth. He spit out the pieces of chipped teeth, and felt for her. She was kneeling beside him, a dreadful sight—shuddering violently, face chalky, cuts black, lips turning gray. Shivers cackled, as if something were settled. Despite himself, Robbie started to cry.

"Secrets," Shivers whispered. "So many secrets."

Fristeen grasped Robbie's arm and tried to stand, but she was too weak to lift him.

"Just lies, like Mom said," Shivers hissed. "Fristeen's here because of you."

Shivers was right, Robbie knew. He'd as soon die here. But Fristeen— He'd delivered her to Shivers. His dream had come true.

"Dreams of the condemned," Shivers said with feeling. "Pitiful ghosts. It's just between us—your tears, your shame. No one will ever see the two of you again."

Robbie heard Fristeen sobbing. She was giving up, too. She collapsed beside him, her thin frame shaking. He was sorry, so sorry—

A terrible roar—some new fury of wind overhead. And then the storm tore apart. Robbie saw midnight and moonlight with snow circling down. And through that sudden corridor a dim figure came floating: Hands with his candles lit, high above the trees.

Robbie's heart leaped.

Hands tilted his rack, steam jetting from his nose.

An eddy shrieked in Robbie's face. "Haven't you learned?"

But Robbie raised himself through Shivers' fierce coilings as Hands' blue shadow hovered above. He grabbed Fristeen's arm and helped her up.

"Follow Hands," the voice of the Dream Man spoke through the storm.

The gray ghost turned, antlers flickering like a great candelabra.

"Hands," Robbie said to Fristeen. "See him?"

Shivers laughed. "Hat Rack? What's he doing outdoors?"

"Come on," Robbie said.

"Follow Hands," the Dream Man repeated.

And that's what they did. Hands led the way to the top of the rise, then along its crest. The wind sawed in front of them, teeth digging in, back and forth.

"What are you doing?" Shivers howled in Robbie's face.

Is this the way back?

"That's up to you," the Dream Man said.

Robbie imagined the consuming fire of his dream, and the wind thrashing in his face was, for a moment, flame.

"Rot!" Shivers squalled, incredulous.

Will Fristeen be safe?

"Safe?" Shivers groaned.

"Dawn is waiting," the Dream Man replied.

At that, Shivers howled with mirth and contempt. "You charlatan!" he harangued the Dream Man. "You shameless fake!"

As the ridge tended down, so did Hands. He was gliding now among whipping thickets, a shadow just visible through the flying snow.

"Can you see him?" Fristeen shouted.

"Down there." Robbie pointed. And they descended, hurrying after him.

Shivers swept down, crushing the trees, pulling them up by their roots and hurling them aside. "After all this," he raged, "is there nothing you've learned?"

Robbie shielded his face with the crook of his arm. He looked up just in time to see a large aspen heel back. Its roots raked up mud, and then a black wheel rose. Shivers was a mat of dripping earth, hanging from its arms—two root-nodule eyes, pale and bulging, and a root-spike for a nose. "Hands! Where's Hands," Shivers croaked like a frog.

And when they'd stumbled around the wheel, Hands was lost from view.

"Where is he?" Robbie muttered.

They scanned the stormy woodland in vain. Then they heard a sudden clatter—Hands banging his rack against a tree. And there he was, not far away, halfway up a steep slope, turning to face them through the wind-blown snow.

"There," Fristeen cried out, waving her arms.

Hands bucked his head, faced the slope and rose, tines cleaving the white curtain, white streamers trailing back.

They hurried after him, passed through a low thicket, and started up the steep rise. The storm backed off as they scrambled toward the heights, panting and stumbling. And when they reached the top, Hands was waiting aloft.

Robbie wiped his eyes with his wrist.

"The Two-Tree." He couldn't believe it. "Fristeen—"

She nodded, teeth chattering, and together they drew closer.

The mount looked different in white. But there was no mistaking the tree they knew so well. The pair of boles rose, naked and alone, standing its ground in the eye of the storm. And right at its top was Hands, looking down.

From here, Robbie thought, they could reach the Cabin or find their way back. But when he gazed around, his confidence sank. Shivers had hold of everything. Through the lull in the flurries, you could see the border of Too Far. But the way down to the Pool was clogged with drifts. And the way back was no different. The slope descending to Used-to-Be, the thicket skirting the Great Place— It was all buried in snow. They were stranded and freezing.

Fristeen saw it, too. She hugged him, both shaking badly. *Our journey ends here,* her eyes seemed to say. Two trunks from the same root, alone and bereft, frozen on the border between this world and the next.

"Climb," said the Dream Man.

Climb? Robbie wondered. *What do you mean?* He peered up at Hands, hovering above the topmost branches.

"You will see," said the Dream Man.

The wind was so loud, it hurt his ears. Climb? That was impossible. Wasn't it? He put his hand on the Two-Tree. It was freezing cold. It had no low branches. Just the two entwined boles, twisting as they rose.

"Robbie—" Fristeen called, as if from a distance.

"Climb," the Dream Man repeated.

He put his hand on the bark, lodged his foot in a gap between the trunks, and pulled himself up.

"Robbie!" Fristeen shrieked.

Robbie took a breath.

"Don't be afraid," the Dream Man said.

"Don't be afraid," Robbie said numbly, looking down.

Fristeen was wide-eyed, her shivering face flecked with snow.

He found another toehold and hiked himself up. And another. Then he slipped. But the next one was good. He hugged one trunk, then the other, circling with his left arm, reaching with his right, the ground dropping steadily beneath him. Higher, higher. A flurry of snow matted his face, clouding his sight. He mopped his eyes. The first branch jutted, a few feet above.

"You'll never reach it," Shivers whispered, trying to unnerve him.

Higher, a precarious toehold. Then the branch was before him, and Robbie looped his arm over it. It was thick and stiff. And another higher, and the next, and the next. He reached the place where the two boles drew apart. Hands was leaning to the left, so that's the one Robbie picked. Finding footholds, grabbing on, rising, rising—

Through the veil of flying snow, he could see the Pool now, spectral and shimmering. He reached for the next branch and pulled himself higher, and the next, and the next, working around. There were the Great trees. The crowns were white humps, like giant eggs. Above him, Hands drifted closer, lowering his long face through the blast. His antlers quivered and hummed. Closer he came, and still closer as Robbie rose.

The branches were bendy. Hands was just above. Robbie couldn't climb any higher.

"Now look down," the Dream Man said.

Robbie clung to the swaying bole and searched the forest below.

"What do you see?" the deep voice asked.

The black spruce all moved together, and the white leafy trees, they did as well. This way and that—all the forest was shaking, every tree, every place, all speaking at once. All dim and all white, a sea of confusion. And then through it, a handful of little square lights.

My home, Robbie thought. Its windows were glowing. And through the shifting veil, he could see a car in the drive—a police car, with its colored lights blinking.

"Turn, Robbie, turn."

Above, Hands put his nose to the wind, snorting steam, facing Too Far.

A pair of squares blazed through the spindly spruce. The Cabin, made ready. And a way was clear. On its unexplored side, a ravine led down from the Two-Tree and entered Too Far. It touched a road, white with snow, that Robbie had never known was there—a little winding road that led into the Hollow.

Will you burn us up? Robbie asked.

"Cleanse you. Perfect you," the Dream Man replied.

When?

"Don't test my patience. It must be straightaway."

Is Dawn there, too?

"Dawn is waiting," the Dream Man said.

Robbie turned again, saw the house he and his parents had lived in, and around it other faint lights—a world he barely knew—

"How would we get back?"

"Hands can carry you. If it's the Cabin, you're on your own. Be sure, Robbie. Be sure . . ." The deep voice trailed away.

"Hands—" Robbie gasped. "I can't feel anything."

The furry head dipped, the soft nose drew close. Hands used his breath to warm Robbie's fingers, while his gentle eyes gave Robbie fresh hope.

"Grand," Shivers jeered. "Isn't he grand?" A great blast came charging out of the sky. Then a crack—the branch bearing Robbie's weight gave way. He scrabbled and clinched, swinging over the drop, then pulled himself back and slid down to the next. Down and down, branch after branch, till he was shinning and sliding down the conjoined boles.

His feet touched the ground, and Fristeen's arms found him. As weak as she was, she had to hold him up.

"I know the way," he answered her amazement.

"To the Cabin?"

Robbie caught his breath, nodding. "Dawn is waiting. Or—"

"What?" Her eyes searched him.

"Hands will carry us home."

Fristeen blinked up at the floating head high above. The wind's fury had waned, but the snow was falling thicker than ever.

Robbie stroked her cold cheek with his quaking hand. Her cuts looked purplish against her freezing skin. "You're so beautiful—" He gazed from her face to his hand and then took in their pitiful bodies, all soaked and shuddering. "We have to give up these."

"Robbie—" Fristeen hugged him and then she was crying.

"It's scary—" His voice choked. "I'm really afraid."

She nodded. Then she drew back. "But we're brave," she said ardently. "We're really brave."

Robbie saw the sparkle in her eyes, and then the universe that was theirs—just theirs—burst into sight. Through the ravages of Shivers and the terrible night, poured that golden smile. All the glory of Dawn, unvanquished, rising to bless a new world with its light.

You could choose to leave everything for that— Leave it, or die trying.

He reached for her hand and they started across the mount, headed for the Hollow, and the bed in the Cabin where the transforming flames would blaze.

Hands was with them till they descended into the ravine, then he floated on ahead. The snow in the trough was soft and deep, and they sank and stumbled at every step. The big crosswinds couldn't reach them there, and for a few minutes

238

they imagined that Shivers had left them. But then Fristeen glanced back and shrieked.

His huge visage was right behind them, wilder than ever, lips writhing, making strange gargling sounds.

"There's something in his mouth," Fristeen cried.

They could see white lumps shifting between the bilious lips. And then Shivers hacked and heaved and spit them out. They came tumbling down the ravine like a pack of white spiders, and when they reached Robbie and Fristeen, they leaped and clung to their backs. They had gleaming red eyes, and teeth like glass, and you could feel their legs clawing and scratching, but if you gave them a swat, they crumbled to frost and blew away.

"The road," Robbie yelled.

It appeared just below them, paved with white, veering sharply. And when they reached it and took the curve at full speed, black trees rose up on either side. A great torrent of wind was shaking Too Far, whipping the thin spindles for all they were worth. The road fell before them, diving into the Hollow, and Shivers roared up behind them and dashed them down the slope.

"That's it, boys and girls," he proclaimed. "No more candy and toys—"

Fristeen was rolling over and over. Robbie went up and came down hard. When he stood, he felt an ache through his numbness—his shoulder was crooked, his right arm hung limp. They hurried forward, past a car blanketed with snow.

"For what?" Shivers roared.

"The Cabin!" Fristeen grabbed Robbie, pointing.

Through the quaking trees, an amber beacon shone.

Their eyes met—their freedom was waiting—the moment their dreams had so long foretold.

"For what?" Shivers bellowed.

But they paid no heed. They were racing around to the Cabin's front, splashing madly through the black lagoon.

There it was— The charred walls were caked and sintered with frost. Flames and shadows danced in the panes. Above the snow-covered roof, blue smoke coiled up. A great *crump* sounded, and part of the roof collapsed, taking the stovepipe. There was a crash within, shouts, and then fire blazed up, washing the windows.

"For what!" Shivers screamed. "An idiot smile and a jar full of dreams?"

He burled up behind them and struck them both— one last burst of rage that sent them hurling, and left them sprawled twenty feet from the Cabin door.

It swung open. In the orange and gold light, two dark figures appeared, one behind the other.

Robbie rose to his feet, and so did Fristeen. He fought his fear and clasped her hand. "We're ready," he told them.

They didn't look like gods. They had blankets over their shoulders, and the bigger one's head was no taller than a man's. The smaller cried out, hurried forward and knelt before them.

The blanket opened and wings emerged. They folded around Fristeen. Dawn's features were edged by the fire.

It was Grace, Robbie saw.

"My baby, my baby— How in the world—"

Fristeen's face was glazed with shock. Grace was glowing. She was covered with oil. And her eyes were like nothing Robbie had ever seen: black and wild, mostly pupil, with orange rays around them—like tear tracks or claw marks painted on her cheeks. Fristeen saw the same, and something else. Robbie followed her gaze. There were needles bristling from a tiara of wands circling Grace's head.

The fire swelled inside the Cabin. Giant flames speared through the roof. Scarlet tapers were piercing the walls, sighing and whistling—

"No," Fristeen whimpered. Her head turned and Robbie saw her desperate plea.

But there was no time to react. The man was stepping toward him. Through the gap in his blanket, he was naked to the waist. His chest glinted—like Grace, he was covered with oil and painted strangely, his trunk banded purple and littered with stars. Behind him, the blaze blossomed through the doorway. The Cabin was a furnace, its insides pure flame. The man stooped, his face stubbled black. Then the lips, the smile—all so familiar. And the dream of leaving, dark and gleaming in those distant eyes.

"Robbie," Dad said.

He could barely hear Dad's voice over the rushing. Dad's

arm shifted and something fell at Robbie's feet. In the strobe of light, he saw a crown of birch bark stripped from a Great tree.

Fristeen had hold of Grace's wing. It was a patchwork of lichens and bark, stitched together with green yarn.

The roof collapsed, taking the front wall, and the giant furnace was suddenly a golden mouth opening, chanting, a great song ascendant, swelling triumphant at what it saw in the sky. A dark cloud had drifted over the Hollow, livid with moonlight, and dragonflies arrowed through it from every side. Smoke from the Cabin unfolded great wings that fingered the winds, lifting. And in the center of the billowing cumuli, a glowing cauldron appeared with a crescent of froth, turquoise and lemon, spilling over its rim. The rushing mounted, growing louder and louder as the Dream Man drew near.

Robbie imagined he'd bolted, and Fristeen was with him. Side by side, hands holding tight, they raced toward the flames. But he was moving away from them. Dad had swept him up.

Fristeen was sobbing. Grace held her now. The sound pierced Robbie, and tears welled from deep in his chest. Instead of rising to join the Dream Man and Dawn, they were headed toward the road and the snow-covered car.

He saw Fristeen's eyes seeking him. They gazed at each other, then together, they turned their faces up.

The wings of smoke were no longer soaring. They were teetering, torn to pieces by an angry wind. Drifting feathers were stretching, longer and longer. All the dragonflies had vanished,

and the rushing was dying. As they watched, the smoky ribbons rippled together, weaving a veil across the moon. A night
full of dreams was fading from view. The livid clouds dimmed,
and the cauldron drew back into the depths of the sky. And
all that whistling and huffing from the wind and the flames
turned into one long sigh. The Hollow, the black trees—all of
Too Far—seemed to be grieving. This heaven, this glory, the
promised deliverance—was not to be.

When nothing remained of the Cabin but embers and
chars, the storm left off. The skies were quiet and the earth was
white. The snow-covered woodland seemed at peace. It was the
peace of the dead, for Shivers lay over it, and the bright things
of summer lay buried beneath. High above, a rift in the clouds
let moonlight through. The humped crowns of the Great Place
had all been bridged. The Great roof rose undivided, round
and smooth as a chalky skull—some great creature, perhaps,
that Shivers had eaten.

As their oracle had foreseen, Robbie went away with his
mother. Not long after, Fristeen went to live with a family that
a man in the courthouse gave her. The two children never saw
each other again. It was hard for them both, but time blunted
their pain. They survived, they grew up, they found homes in
the world. But they remembered the summer with each other,
the places they made their own, and the gods they invented.

And the gods remember them.

The northern storms are fierce, and they blow to this day. Winter's cold withers the leaves, and harsh winds rattle the skeletal trees. You would think the last joy in the world had fled.

But beside the dead woodland, life is still stirring. Swirling with breath. A faint hum rides the breeze.

There's a refuge, a place winter hasn't laid waste to. Warmth is protected—steam rises from the peat. Through the whisper of loose crystals and the pulsing gusts— A familiar voice is singing of her endless love. Squeals thread the low hills, frozen in time—the echoes of children daring to wander, a sweeter life in mind. Here at the world's edge, their spirits run naked and free, watched over by gods, immune to the seasons. A place made of equal parts waking and sleep. Where a jay silhouette mounts a turret of cones, sees the first light and shrugs the snow from its wings. A place of mysteries, deep secrets and dreams—where the water flows red and the black trees lean.